SEIZE THE STORM

By Michael Cadnum

SEIZE THE STORM

MICHAEL CADNUM

FARRAR STRAUS GIROUX
NEW YORK

Farrar Straus Giroux Books for Young Readers
175 Fifth Avenue, New York 10010

Distributed in Canada by D&M Publishers, Inc.
Printed in the United States of America
Designed by Alexander Garkusha
First edition, 2012
1   3   5   7   9   10   8   6   4   2

macteenbooks.com

Library of Congress Cataloging-in-Publication Data
Cadnum, Michael.
     Seize the storm / Michael Cadnum. — 1st ed.
        p.   cm.
     Summary: On a pleasure cruise in the Pacific, seventeen-year-old Susannah,
her parents, seventeen-year-old cousin Martin, and eighteen-year-old crew
member Axel face off against seventeen-year-old Jeremy, a drug lord's son, and
hired killers Elwood and fifteen-year-old Shako.
     ISBN 978-0-374-36705-3 (hardcover)
     ISBN 978-1-4299-5488-4 (e-book)
     [1. Adventure and adventurers—Fiction. 2. Boats and boating—Fiction.
3. Criminals—Fiction. 4. Dogs—Fiction. 5. Pacific Ocean—Fiction.] I. Title.

PZ7.C11724Sie 2012
[Fic]—dc22

                                                                    2011020865

For Sherina

A gull—
so far
from home—
home

SEIZE THE STORM

THE AIRCRAFT FLEW EASTWARD, its airspeed steady at one hundred and ninety miles per hour, one thousand feet above the Pacific, a red and white twin-engine customized de Havilland, outfitted for water takeoff and landing.

Jeremy switched on the radio again. *"Witch Grass, this is Red Bird, do you copy?"*

He said this over and over, nothing but faint white noise in his headset.

Jeremy turned off the transmitter. He liked using the radio, getting into that high-plains drawl pilots used, roger this, roger that. But you couldn't have a conversation with nothing. Well, you could, but you'd be like one of those meth heads outside the video arcade in Kapaa, talking nonstop, no one listening.

Jeremy's dad was a warlord criminal. Through minions, he dealt drugs to these ravaged souls, but his dad told Jeremy to stay away from both the dealers and their customers. He wanted Jeremy to learn from the predators at the top of the food chain, of which Elwood was the prime example.

Jeremy peeled the wrapper off a ProteinPlus bar, offering it to Elwood, who was piloting the plane, and then he unwrapped a bar for himself.

"Better wake Shako," said Elwood, chewing hard around the wad of protein bar. "Make sure he eats one, too."

Sure, wake Shako and feed him, thought Jeremy with an ironic smile. Like feeding a tarantula. He would wake Shako in a moment—you had to prepare yourself for the encounter.

"Fly out there with Elwood and don't come back without the money," his dad had said. He had been slumped in a chair beside his crumpled bedding two days after a hernia operation, the pain medication wearing off.

This was the first time Ted Tygart had ordered his son on an assignment, the first time Jeremy had gone on a non-drill operation with Elwood, and Jeremy dreaded disappointing either man.

Elwood piloted the airplane in his aloha shirt and Sleeping Giant Spa baseball cap, cargo pants, and black combat boots, a rangy man with red hair on his head and curly red hair on his arms. He needed a shave—he had been at the controls for more than six hours.

The aircraft had a range of over two thousand sea miles, thanks to auxiliary fuel reserves. Still, the plane could not go on like this forever, and besides, they would have to swing well to the north to avoid the storm heading this way.

A transponder on the missing vessel was sending out a location indicator, showing where the lost craft was, and that gave Elwood an illuminated image to follow on the radar screen. But it was very hard to translate the bright dot on the cockpit panel, a pulsing sore, to an actual position on the sea.

"I'm going to circle," said Elwood, speaking easily over the sound of the engine.

He was not asking for permission, exactly, but the boss's son got a little respect. Jeremy drew a little circle with his finger and nodded. These protein bars were full of flavor, but they stuck your teeth together.

The aircraft banked, slipping northward. Then they looped west. Jeremy kept his eyes on the tilting expanse before him, the Pacific a glittering slab, nothing visible but the skittering, fugitive ghost of the airplane's shadow as the sun rose.

Jeremy slipped his BlackBerry out of his pocket and read the last message from Kyle. *im KIA sht/Pl 2 bi me lzr trfd.*

Even by the standards of compressed text messages, this communication had been terse. But the meaning was unmistakable, given Jeremy's experience in figuring out messages from Kyle Molline. Kyle was always laughing, playing catch, fooling around.

I am killed in action—shot. Paul too, by me. Laser is terrified.

Laser was the dog, the three-year-old German shepherd that was supposed to keep Kyle company and act as backup security in case something went wrong. Jeremy liked Laser very much. He and Kyle played Frisbee with the dog, but Elwood hated the animal, and the dog hated him.

This message had to be an exaggeration. Kyle couldn't be dead, as in actually dead. He was fooling around—but they could not be sure.

"Can I look at the gun?" asked Jeremy.

"Sure," said Elwood.

But he gave a little tilt of his head and a set of his mouth that let Jeremy know: be careful.

He leaned down and picked up the MP5 from the floor of the aircraft, down there with the canvas backpack of emergency gear—a flashlight, a flare gun and an air horn, and a zipped-up black gun case, part of Elwood's personal arsenal.

The Heckler & Koch had a teardrop-shaped safety switch on the side and diagrams showing the rate of fire settings. The full automatic setting was a stream of bullets like red footballs. The barrel would get so hot the operator needed to wear protective gloves. The canvas pack contained a pair of Blackhawk Hot Ops gloves ready and waiting. Elwood had loaned the weapon to Jeremy for practice outings, cutting plumeria branches to pieces.

Property San Jose PD was etched along the stock. It had been stolen right out of a police yard vehicle by one of Elwood's former associates.

"I have two clips down there in the bag," said Elwood, "along with some other stuff. And Shako has a couple extra clips, along with his own ammo. Don't you, Shako?"

This last was louder than the rest, and Jeremy could feel Shako stirring in the rear of the passenger compartment.

Shako wore wraparound Cartier sunglasses, black Noko denims, and Black Mamba edition Nikes. He had close-cropped brown hair like a scrub pad, and was tanned dark by the Hawaiian sunlight. Shako was fifteen years old and had killed people. Jeremy understood that he had taken lives for hire in Richmond,

California, where he was from, and on the high seas off the Big Island and Maui. Two years younger than Jeremy, he was a professional.

Shako lifted his sunglasses, revealing green eyes. He stared right back, an interesting experience for Jeremy. His eyes were two decimal points, vision-holes. They gave no evidence of feeling or personality. Shako had *smack down* tattooed on his right arm, and something in Chinese tattooed on his left arm.

"You woke him up, Elwood," said Jeremy, to place the blame where it belonged.

"Sorry, there, Mr. Quinn," said Elwood. "I was going to ask if you were hungry. Jeremy brought us some snacks."

Elwood was maybe forty years old and he called Shako "mister." When you were a killer like Shako, you got respect.

Shako looked at the protein bar Jeremy was offering and reached out and took it.

It was like the time an elephant took a peanut from Jeremy's hand, outside the new Safeway in Lihue. It was a surprise acceptance, the trunk curling around and tucking the peanut into the great mammal's unexpectedly tiny mouth. Jeremy had felt honored.

There was a tug at his sleeve, and to his surprise Shako was handing a protein bar of his own between the seats, an exchange, a CLIF Organic ZBar.

"Thanks, Shako," said Jeremy.

Behind his sunglasses, Shako was tightening his lips together, not a smile exactly, but close.

Jeremy was surprised. A gesture of friendship from Shako.

He could hardly wait to tell Kyle that maybe Shako was human.

Because Kyle was alive. He had to be. You could talk to Kyle, not like hanging out with Shako, afraid he might take offense and shoot your head off.

"Take a look, to the south, Jeremy," Elwood said, pointing. "One of those yachts your dad always wanted."

He banked the plane and Jeremy used the binoculars, taking in the yacht and the spacious, metallic ocean.

"It would be nice to capture that," said Elwood musingly. "It would sure make your dad happy. I'd be pleased just to set foot on a vessel like that."

That was one more problem with Elwood. He was civil, but he insinuated his way into your thoughts and generally did things his way. Even bringing Shako along had been his idea. What was he talking about now, stealing yachts?

Not one of them was paying that much attention when they hit the thing. One moment Elwood was taking a drink of vitaminwater and Jeremy was using his teeth to open the CLIF bar and Shako was settling back down in the back, like an eel back into his shadows.

With a startling whiplash snap, the Plexiglas windscreen took a hit, cracks all over the surface, and there was a simultaneous shock that traveled along the framework of the aircraft.

Jeremy had sometimes wondered what people did during a plane crash. Did they say anything, or did they spend their last moments with silently gritted teeth, making sure their seat belts were snug? Or did people who never gave a thought to God suddenly think hard about the Almighty?

Or maybe people didn't really do very much at all, too alarmed and too busy inwardly bracing for impact.

Because that was basically what Jeremy did, and Elwood, too, as though flying straight down like this was what they had planned. Only Shako, the professional killer, was wailing, like a hurt animal, or actually more like a hurt and stricken person, stuck in a crack and the crack closing, about to die.

THE SUN WAS UP.

The sky was bare of cloud, a few lingering stars above, and a half-moon aglow. The sea was calm, too, easy swells dimpled with eddies as the vessel cut through the water. They were a long way from San Francisco, their home port, and not as far from Honolulu, their destination.

Susannah saw the threat, an object half submerged in the water.

"Slow down!" she called to her mother at the helm of *Athena's Secret*, and the yacht powered down, the port and starboard engines both shifting to idle.

The forward momentum of the craft gradually decelerated, and Susannah seized the boat hook and got ready to fend off what could be real danger—maybe a chunk of freighter debris or a floating explosive.

The ocean was not clean. Objects floated in the waves, and not simply the incidental plastic bottles. Miles of fishing wire floated below the surface, threatening to befoul propellers, and carpets of nurdles—raw plastic that had been flushed down factory drains—could easily jam a rudder.

To make matters worse, craggy timbers and drifting

furniture had been known to damage ships in collisions at sea, and there were legends of spike-encrusted, superannuated mines that escaped from storage and swept the currents, blindly seeking targets.

Leonard was on the lookout for salvage, or what he called "waveson," the old term for floating wreckage that could be lawfully collected and that belonged to the finder. In the unlikely event of the discovery of a craft that was abandoned and derelict, Leonard and his crew could claim a salvage reward from the owners, and could claim the entire cargo if no lawful owners could be discovered.

This whimsical adventurism added zest to the cruise. So far, the only useful flotsam they had hooked from the water had been an Igloo ice chest.

Susannah thrust the long boat hook across the water. The pole had a brass crook at the end, like a shepherd's crook. When she reached the lunging metal thing, she set her feet. Using all her strength, she fended the object away, fighting it off. An oil barrel. The logo was vivid red and gold, *Shell*, barely corroded by the sea.

It was not easy—the sea forced the unsteady, heavy drum back toward the wooden hull—and it was only with a great effort that Susannah was able to compel the barrel far enough away that the ship's wake fanned out to meet it and the danger bobbed past them to the east.

Susannah put the boat hook back where it belonged, just under the gunwale along the inside of the yacht.

"Cruise speed," she called, and her mother throttled up,

the yacht's velocity increasing to ten knots—their normal speed in fair weather.

Over two thousand miles from the Mainland, the birds had been a friendly albatross and a team of male frigate birds, large fowl with graceful wings and long, cutlass-fierce beaks. These were the young males who had not found a mate for the summer, so they ranged the ocean in groups of threes or fours, companionable rivals, enjoying their ability to loft upward with the wind and snap sea bass out of the water.

Now these birds had disappeared, except for a remnant few, circling high in the vault of the sky. This far out at sea, she did not expect to see a wandering gull—gulls couldn't drink salt water, and the only gull out here would be lost, or on his way back to land as fast as he could fly.

There had been a cascade of flying fish at first light, the first flying fish of the voyage, and Susannah had a surprise for her cousin Martin.

But now the only signs of life were the contrails of jetliners, blurred slashes far above. And just then a new arrival—a red and white airplane, far to the north.

The aircraft was heading east, too far away to make a sound. As Susannah watched, it turned gracefully in a different direction. Something about the far-off airplane puzzled Susannah, and she felt the first beginnings of concern.

Safety was on everyone's mind. Central America's drug wars had spilled over onto the sea, and as far north as Juneau the Coast Guard had been in running battles with ships laden with illegal cargo. Pleasure craft had been captured routinely by pirates, and this family voyage might prove to be reckless.

At least the blue shark that had been trailing them in recent days was reliable. He appeared with the rising sun, the creature showing off the way an F-16 buzzing a stadium showed off, demonstrating his powers.

What would you tell me, she wondered.

She listened to the silence. Martin joked that she was crazy, believing that she could hear what animals were thinking. Martin was gentle, even when he was being critical.

So maybe she was a little foolish. But surely she could hear what the shark was obsessing about, that long-living spear, blue as any Pacific swell on his topside and sky-pale beneath, so no creature below could see him coming.

Hunger was all she sensed from him. But nothing like human hunger—the real thing, primordial and, except for brief intervals, everlasting.

Susannah had worked recent summers at the Marine Mammal Center north of San Francisco, helping to nurse harbor seals who had been cut by boat propellers or snagged by fish nets, abscesses in their fins. Or worse—sometimes the animals had been shot.

Now Susannah went aft, to be closer to her mother, Claudette, and switched on the marine scanner, listening to ship-to-ship chatter, except there wasn't any this early in the morning, just the empty hiss of static, gentle and not quite reassuring.

Susannah asked, "Can you smell it in the air?"

Her mother was at the wheel, smoking. Of course she couldn't smell anything, inhaling cigarette smoke unapologetically and moodily, staring at Susannah as she shook her head no. She seemed to still be brooding over a conversation they'd had earlier.

"The air smells salty, like the beach," said Susannah.

Open ocean smelled like fresh laundry, whole sheets of it, wide and clean. It shouldn't smell like this.

This thick, brackish air meant a storm was coming.

"I KNEW ALL ABOUT YOUR FATHER and that woman," Claudette said at last, resuming their conversation from earlier after the long, edgy break. "You weren't telling me any news."

Susannah groaned aloud. She wasn't given to silent exasperation. When she was unhappy, people knew it.

She shouldn't have mentioned the subject. She should have kept her mouth shut. Who cared about extramarital affairs these days? She called her parents by their first names. They were a modern family.

"You knew about it?"

"He told me," Claudette replied.

Claudette had a way of standing that looked as though she had an attitude of prideful dismissiveness toward everything around her, one foot forward, the other at an angle, one hand on her hip.

The truth was that she had injured her right knee falling from a horse as a teenager. The knee was chronically weak, and she stood and walked in a manner calculated to disguise this flaw.

So why the long sulk? wondered Susannah.

"Claudette," she said, " I have trouble believing that Dad told you everything."

"He told me he saw her, and he told me it was innocent." Claudette tossed the cigarette away, and it flew wide, over the side of the yacht into the sea. This bothered Susannah, her mother using the Pacific as an ashtray.

"It didn't look innocent," said Susannah.

Her mother was proud—arrogant, even, with good reason. She was smart and good-looking. Susannah figured her mother deserved better than a cheating husband.

"Where were they?" came the question again. They had been through all this.

"In Oakland, at Jack London Square," Susannah said, "near the ferry station."

"When?" This time more sharply. Her mother might have hidden deficiencies, Susannah knew, but she had hidden powers, too. She got what she wanted.

"A month ago," said Susannah. "Maybe five weeks."

"Just like he told me," said her mother, perhaps betraying just a small amount of relief.

Susannah gave a shrug.

"He told me Michelle was going to work for the FBI. It was a farewell lunch."

Susannah waved her hand OK. She wanted to drop the subject. Maybe it was a relief to figure out now that her dad had not been cheating.

Claudette thought for a while. "Are you sure it was Michelle?"

What an odd question, thought Susannah. If she already knew, why was she asking? Another hidden weakness. But she felt a little compassion for Claudette. After all, they were talking about marital dynamite. "No one looks like her, with that mustard-yellow hair, or wears those—"

She made a gesture across her upper thigh.

No one else sports those unstylish but never completely out-of-date short skirts, she meant. Except her father's old legal secretary, his former and now maybe not-so-former girlfriend. Susannah had told Martin about the sighting, and he had suggested not mentioning it, at least not until the voyage was over and they were safely berthed in Honolulu.

But her mother had been sharing the predawn watch with her daughter, and the warm air was so sweet that her mother had started bragging about what great luck she had enjoyed all her life. This had to be a lie, or at least an exaggeration. The last year had been one slump after another, with the family stockbroker finally quitting and leaving for the Bahamas. And for some reason Susannah had felt like pricking that air of self-congratulation, cutting her mother down.

Claudette lit a fresh cigarette. Someone else was awake now. He was moving around below, the wooden deck communicating the movement of a human body over the vibration of the engines. Someone big, Martin probably, tiptoeing forward to the galley, where Leonard, her father, was probably already up, too, preparing the ingredients for his mysteriously delicious hot cocoa.

"This is a bad time," said Claudette, "to even think about divorcing your father."

Susannah put her hands over her eyes. No, no, no, she wanted to protest. This was not what she was suggesting.

Claudette could survive a divorce emotionally intact. She was good-looking in an athletic, silver-tipped way—tall, size sixteen, and with the posture and shape to go with it, aside from her old injury. Dad, however, would be wrecked by a breakup. He was an affable man who couldn't sleep without pills, a man who loved life but suffered emotional downturns in broad sweeps of feeling.

When his own father died he had sat in a darkened room for a week and lost ten pounds. When Claudette's mom died, Claudette wore a black scarf and bought an iPhone. Both of Susannah's parents were genuine and loving, but her dad was an animated bear, and her mom was an ocelot.

"Our stock portfolio is dust," said Mom now, "and our money market is down to pennies." She spoke as though to herself, closing one eye against the smoke, keeping the cigarette in her mouth, looking tough and ready for anything. The cigarette bobbed up and down when she added, "Divorce would be a financial H-bomb for both of us."

"What are we going to do about Axel?" asked Susannah, wanting to seek some common cause with her mother.

"Anything you like," said Claudette.

Axel had been coming on to Susannah, not overtly, but with a quiet, possessive air that bothered her. It was hard to avoid someone on a yacht in the middle of the Pacific Ocean.

Axel was the only paid crew member, an eighteen-year-old with a lot of sea experience and a high opinion of his powers. Susannah was a year younger than Axel, with a lot less know-how, and she had to admit that Axel had sex appeal. He didn't talk much to her, and she did not mind. Axel liked talking to men, showing off. He just looked at her and smiled, sticking his chin out.

"I'll tell him to leave you alone, if you want," said Claudette.

"I'd feel embarrassed."

Claudette conceded this possibility with a contemplative smile.

Susannah liked this about her mother. She had a way of sighing that made everyone around her feel like failures, but she got the point of things quickly. Claudette had been a manager for Macy's, before the business collapse cost her the job, and she had always been hurrying to a meeting with the Talbots agent or the Cole Haan rep. Claudette knew how to deal with people.

"We've all gone salmon fishing with Axel a few times," Claudette said. She got the gold Dunhill lighter out of her pants pocket, flicked it, and lit yet another cigarette, the burst of Marlboro menthol smoke vanishing into the air. But Susannah caught the scent of it, raw perfume, toxic but almost desirable, even to someone who had never smoked.

Claudette drew on her cigarette and gave a sideways toss of her head, an unspoken *Never mind Axel.*

"Have you been watching that airplane?" Claudette was asking now.

"Heading east, and then heading north," said Susannah. "For the last ten, fifteen minutes."

Claudette had the big Pentax binoculars up to her eyes, focusing. She kept one hand on the helm and manipulated the binoculars easily with the other.

She said, "Now I can't see it—like it vanished."

MARTIN CLIMBED OUT ON DECK. Susannah wondered why guys like Martin always looked great in the morning, fresh out of bed.

He said her name, and she said his in return, casual and cheerful like it was no big deal, but for her, seeing him after an absence was always a forceful moment. Martin had a way of changing things, shifting the mood, making it better. If you could fall in love with your first cousin, that's what she was doing.

Martin had thick auburn hair and a hale, easygoing manner that could be welcoming or thoughtful, depending on his mood. This morning he wore army-green shorts and a Scripps Oceanography T-shirt, his feet thrust into a pair of Top-Siders. He had studied tide pools and sea currents at Scripps last summer, had taken scuba lessons, too, and had come back talking about plankton and carbon dioxide levels.

He was in love with everything about the ocean, and Susannah envied him his joy. Getting Martin's mind off a recent tragic incident he had witnessed was one of the main reasons for the voyage, aside from giving Leonard one more chance to skipper the yacht he and his wife could no longer afford.

It wasn't easy to climb up from belowdecks carrying hot drinks, the deck canting and shifting every moment—even under engine power she was a frisky vessel. It was like Martin to show up with something people wanted, at just the right moment. Now he carried two blue mugs of Leonard's cocoa. There was the smell of frying fish in the air from the galley.

"Thank you, Martin," Claudette said, and you could hear in her voice how glad she was to be talking to someone who was not a problem, and not a messenger of trouble. Just a pleasant, agreeable person, someone Mom was glad to have in the family.

"Martin, I collected a specimen for you," Susannah said.

She said this as though she was offhand, but the truth was she was excited.

"Another bird picture?" he inquired eagerly.

She had gotten pretty good at snapping pictures of the albatross that had winged along in their wake until this morning.

"You were telling me you'd never seen one before."

"One what?" asked Martin, enjoying this, wanting to make a game of it.

"Does the word *exocoetidae* mean anything to you?" she asked.

"Really!" he exclaimed.

She liked to spring scientific words on Martin, to confound him, even if she had to more or less make them up. She referred to Leonard's chronic back trouble mock seriously as "vertebral vertebratis," and when a movie made her teary she called it "cinematic lachrymosis."

"Take a look in the collecting bucket."

She had hoped to see him pleased, and she was not disappointed.

Even though they were both seventeen and shared a quality of family good looks and intelligence, she felt very much more likely to succeed than Martin. Succeed—but not find happiness. She saw herself running a veterinary clinic in Mill Valley or Orinda in a few years, the sort of vet who cured feline leukemia before lunch and then drove out to a horse ranch to see how that new thoroughbred foal was coming along.

She expected Martin to be caught up in some sort of marine discipline, studying the life cycle of the sea cucumber. But he would be loved and admired by his colleagues and have many friends. Susannah knew she was the sort of reasonably good-looking person who would have trouble getting dates, except with guys like Axel.

She wanted to change all that.

"There was a school of them," said Susannah. "Escaping a hungry tuna, I suppose. This one hopped up on deck."

"A black-winged flying fish," said Martin.

"A lot of people," said Susannah, "are disappointed how small they are."

"He's enormous," said Martin.

He gave her his smile and she felt it all the way through.

She made up songs. Nobody knew this about her. She talked without hesitation and was free with her tartest opinions. But her songwriting was strictly private, music in her own head. This was what she would like to put into a song right then: the sunlight on the water, the way Martin gave his silent laugh.

The fish was aware of Martin's shadow and splashed, not frightened so much as showing off, discouraging a prospective predator from assuming he would make an easy breakfast.

He gave the fish an appreciative moment, admiring the animal as it scouted around and around in the interior of the plastic bucket. Then Martin picked up the container and tossed the fish into the ocean.

He was rewarded by the sight of the fish leaping and skittering across the waves, looking like a dragonfly granted superpowers, thought Susannah, or a sparrow that had adapted to a watery existence.

She sipped her cocoa and thought that instant into a song, too, privately, the tune in her head. *I'm free again, but I'm yours.*

I'm yours forever.

You could use *forever* in a song, she knew, a word too sentimental to break into everyday speech.

The cocoa was delicious, served up in the appealing, heavy-duty mugs. The mugs were part of the set that Leonard had ordered especially designed by a studio in Copenhagen, back when he had money to burn. They were light blue in color, and on the side of each mug was a picture of the yacht that they were sailing on, *Athena's Secret*, with her sails set, the artwork cobalt blue, with dark blue waves parting around the prow.

"I'm afraid a storm's coming, Martin," Susannah said.

Martin looked upward at the blue sky. Then he gave her a glance of friendly skepticism.

"Believe me," said Susannah.

Martin headed back below again. He returned at once, with his Sony notebook computer, and found a place under the flat canvas awning that shaded the helm and where the flip-up screen didn't have to compete with the glare off the sea. In addition to the classic spoked wheel, the helm was equipped with padded benches, running forward and aft, and side tables for beverages and snacks.

The yacht had shipboard Wi-Fi through a small gray dish on the foremast, and they got communication by digital telephone through the same technology. If the dish got knocked down or the generator blew, they'd have trouble, but for now the entire world was just a power button away.

Leonard joined them right then, smelling of aftershave and beaming at life in general, a forceful, genial man. He was dressed in his customary fair-weather outfit—a Ralph Lauren polo shirt, seersucker pants, and a pair of well-worn Dubarry deck shoes. His short hair was dark, just flecked with gray, and he had profound dark eyebrows. His face and arms gleamed with sunblock lotion. His dermatologist had burned off a basal cell carcinoma from his forearm the winter before.

In years gone by, Leonard Burgess had been on the Coastal Commission appointed by the governor, honored for his business success and campaign contributions. Susannah knew that those days were over.

"Kippers!" he exclaimed. "I've fried us all a batch of delicious smoked herring."

Her father was a generous man, and he liked people to be

happy. But sometimes his choice of menus left something to be desired. Martin and Susannah gave each other a glance of mock horror. *Kippers*, Martin echoed in silent dismay.

"Susannah's right," said Martin.

"About what?" asked Leonard.

Martin turned his computer so they could all look at the lurid squiggles of the isobars across a map of the Pacific, the scarlet outline of tempest.

"That," said Leonard, "looks like fun."

MARTIN WAS HAPPY.

He loved stepping out on deck and seeing how much bigger the sky always was—every time—than you could imagine it in your mind.

He liked talking with Susannah, and he liked the way she sipped her cocoa, daintily, finding it too hot and then not too hot—just right.

But despite the cocoa and the breathtaking disclosure of the flying fish, things were not as they should be.

Claudette went below shortly, taking her mug of hot cocoa. You could hear her cabin door, feel it shut hard under your feet. She was both tough and stylish, and wore sunny pastels, oversize shirts with sleeves she rolled up, summery pants that fit her perfectly. When Claudette showed up, people acted and thought a little bit smarter, and when she left everyone slouched.

Maybe the smell of frying kippers that wafted out from belowdecks was not the best scent in the world just then.

Leonard gave his daughter a questioning glance.

"She OK?"

Susannah offered up a shrug of incomprehension that satisfied Dad. Martin, though, could see that Susannah was going out of her way to avoid admitting that Claudette was not OK.

Susannah was thin and pretty, with hair that looked sable in morning light, butterscotch in the afternoon. She kept her hair in low-maintenance tails—pigtails, ponytails, multiple extensions that stuck out where they would. His cousin was fond of clothes with single bold stripes up and down the sleeve and along the pant leg. Now she was wearing a blouse that made her look like a crossing guard, a yellow stripe across her body.

"We'll all feel better," Uncle Leonard was saying, "when we get nutrified."

When they ate, he meant.

Leonard coined words like this, his version of being funny. Taking the helm was making sure that the yacht was fully helmitized, and polishing the brass fittings throughout the vessel he called brass-imization.

Martin had to concede that some mature person might find Leonard just a little tedious, but to a young nephew he was a joy. Leonard liked himself, and because he thought most people resembled him in some way, he liked most people, too.

"Hey, it's our first mate," said Leonard as Axel made his appearance on deck.

Axel Owen used a towel to rub the top of his close-cropped head. Axel wasn't the sort of guy who bothered with *good morning* or even *hi*, but he gave a nod to Martin.

Axel was wearing a pair of Diesel denims and a blue

Tommy Bahamas half-zip sweatshirt with the sleeves cut off and left artfully ragged. He radiated a quality of masculine self-assurance so keen that even Uncle Leonard wanted to impress him.

Axel said, "Morning, Skipper."

Martin knew a lot of men like Axel, and you could read them like the ingredients on the back of a bottle. But Axel knew boats, and he was physically tough. Martin liked Axel well enough, but if he had to fight Axel, he would find something to hit him with.

Leonard was the owner and the captain, but he wasn't really a hands-on guy. That fell to Axel and to Martin, because Leonard, for all his enthusiasm and experience, had a bad back, injured moving a pot of sago palms around his patio ten years earlier—although he liked to say he hurt it playing free safety for Cal football. Leonard had actually played practice-squad football for Cal—Martin had looked him up on the University of California Golden Bear Web site.

"It was a quiet night," said Susannah, but she made no move to go below, drinking her cocoa and watching Axel take the helm and up the throttle to fifteen knots. Susannah hated to so much as glance in Axel's direction, but sometimes she couldn't help it.

"Any luck?" asked Leonard.

By *any luck* he meant: had they found anything valuable?

"There was an airplane," added Susannah. "I think it was looking for something."

"Did you check the emergency channel?" asked Axel.

"Mom did," answered Susannah.

"What kind of plane was it?" asked Leonard.

"Seaplane, fairly large, twin engines," said Susannah.

"What kind of weapons do we have on board?" asked Axel.

"I took care of us," said Leonard. "No need to worry."

"We have a Remington twelve-gauge," said Susannah. "But Leonard is so cautious about guns that he keeps the Remington hidden in one overhead bin and the ammo in another, and he hides the keys, too."

Leonard nodded his head.

"Besides," said Susannah, "Leonard's preferred weapons would be brass cannons and harpoons."

"Maybe cutlasses," agreed Leonard with a laugh.

"But I wonder," said Axel.

"Yes," said Susannah. "I'm nervous, too."

She meant to prick Axel a little about feeling apprehensive. But it was true.

MARTIN SHIELDED HIS EYES and looked north. There was no sign of any aircraft now.

On the first day out of San Francisco they had hoisted the genoa—the big foresail—and the sail had torn, flapping and fluttering noisily, until the huge quantity of Dacron canvas had been hauled in by Martin and Axel while Susannah mastered the helm.

Axel was supposedly skilled at stitching canvas, but he had made no move to repair the sail, and when Leonard questioned this, he had said, simply, "When we reach the trade winds, we can sail."

This was reasonable. The prevailing winds they had faced up until now were out of the west. Engine power was easier. That and Leonard's preference for a steady speed, right into the wind, and ample fuel supplies for the engines made this the choice. The engine could not be run at top speed for any length of time, however, and needed frequent transfusions of Pennzoil Marine motor oil to keep from overheating.

But Martin felt that some of the romance of sail was missing, and he knew that Leonard felt this, too, despite himself, and when the prevailing winds began to come out of the east, Martin looked forward to a mainsail bellying in the breeze.

Now Axel turned up the marine scanner so he could get a dose of chitchat—Martin caught the phrase *they got berthing issues big-time*. Axel had a tattoo of a fist on his upper right arm, and Martin thought that was a pretty stupid image to have tattooed on your body. Especially a bunched, angry-looking fist like the one Axel had, with his T-shirts all carefully shorn of their sleeves so you could not avoid seeing it.

"That shark still wants to take a bite out of you," said Susannah, looking right at Axel.

Axel didn't even bother to smile, using a pink rag to wipe down the wooden spokes of the helm. He had complained that Claudette and Susannah left hand cream and sunscreen on the wood.

"I'd choke it," said Axel, "going down."

Then Susannah went below.

"Maybe you could cast a line for the shark, Martin," said Leonard. "Put a New York steak on a four-inch hook. We've got some four-hundred-pound monofilament line—what do you think?" He glanced around, a guy seeking approval from other guys. "Give it a surprise, use the gaff hooks on it, get him on deck and—"

He made a motion, smiting an invisible shark.

He opened the lazarette, the storage compartment on deck where the first aid kit and other emergency gear were kept. The bright yellow raincoats were rolled tightly, and Leonard shook one out. The hooded fluorescent garment had a heavy-duty black zipper, several straps and pockets, and a waterproof transmitter—someone lost overboard in poor visibility might be easily found again.

Leonard held the vinyl jacket up to his front like a department store shopper posing with a new raincoat. The sight of this garment with all its pockets and fastenings for flashlights, flare guns, and whistles made Martin feel that maybe foul weather at sea was a more serious challenge than he had thought.

"Weather-resistant gloves, upward-floating flashlights," Leonard was saying, not talking to anyone in particular, taking an inventory of their disaster readiness. "You can die of hypothermia," he added, "right on board a ship, if you get soaked."

"Won't happen, Skipper," said Axel.

"But the point is," said Leonard, "there is danger involved in powering our way into a big scarlet patch on the weather map." He sounded pleased with the prospect.

"Doesn't bother me," said Axel.

"It's hazardous," said Martin, feeling a trace of disquiet, "but it's not certain destruction, right?"

They took their places around the dining table, leaving Axel at the helm.

The saloon table could be removed and stored when it was

not being used, but it was often left in place. Crew members used the table for catching up on their reading or for tapping out e-mail on their laptops, and this was where they played cutthroat Scrabble. The yacht had a single main cabin, with sleeping quarters arranged off the main saloon and the galley well forward. The quarters themselves were small but pleasant, with doors that closed securely.

The smell of fried fish was strong.

"Uncle Leonard," Martin said. He stopped there and had to gather his resolve. Something about the smiling, energetic man was slightly intimidating right then. "Maybe I could just have one of those frozen muffins."

Instead of the fish, he meant.

"I thought you liked my cooking, Martin," said Leonard.

"I love your fried fish," said Martin. "And your oyster stew, and your turkey and bell pepper hash, and—everything. But those muffins are special."

Leonard lifted a hand off the table, an unspoken insistence, *have a couple of herrings*, that Martin ignored.

"I could just pop a muffin in the microwave," suggested Martin.

Martin got his muffin, served up warm on a plate.

The sleeve of Susannah's jacket brushed his arm as she served him, a muffin for both cousins.

As he ate the delicious blueberry-flavored treat, he reached a point at the center of the muffin where it was still frozen, a small star of unheated substance that was cold on his tongue.

How complicated would it be, he wondered, to fall in love with Susannah?

Sometimes Martin sensed someone's attention, a weight angling in on his own awareness, like the chill from an open freezer. He felt it now and glanced over at Claudette.

Claudette was watching Martin, and not simply looking at him, but reading him, like a news anchor scanning the teleprompter. Martin could see the advantage of experience and a lifetime of developing managerial skills. Claudette could guess what was happening before it was even an actual event. She liked him, he knew, but would not welcome the complication of a shipboard romance between cousins.

"Martin, how are you and Axel getting along?" Claudette was asking.

Martin recognized family cipher when he heard it. Axel was a potential rival, Claudette meant.

"I get along with everyone," said Martin.

Susannah broke her own muffin neatly, calculating how to pull it apart so that, experimentally, she could fit it exactly together again—which she proceeded to do.

"That's the way to be," said Leonard.

"But if you always avoid conflict," said Susannah, "you have to spend a life in retreat."

"Not your problem, Susannah," said Leonard with a smile.

Susannah gave a smile in return, mock irritation. It was hard to be annoyed at Leonard.

The vessel moaned, a quiet sound that came from within the keel and resulted in a series of whispered reports through her length, the joints and strakes stirring under the grip of the sea.

Leonard gave another smile—knowing and a little scary.

THE AIRCRAFT flew straight down for a long time.

Shako stopped yelling when the plane stopped its power dive toward the Pacific.

He wasn't embarrassed at first because he wasn't aware that he was the only one crying out. The engines made a very deep, baritone noise, a sound so deafening that a smaller noise, like a human screaming for his life, could not be clearly heard. Or so he hoped.

After what had seemed like a very long time, Elwood pulled the aircraft out of its dive, with the wave tops streaking past just below the pontoons, a white blur. Shako could believe, tentatively, that they were not all about to smash into the ocean.

"You OK?" Elwood was asking, first Jeremy and then Shako. Shako looked down to check his own crotch. To his great relief he had not peed himself.

Elwood's face with its red eyebrows under his visored cap was looking right at Shako, and Shako felt sheepish now, embarrassed.

He wanted to ask what had happened. Maybe someone had

shot at them from an unseen aircraft, or a drone had shot a burst at them. You heard about such things. Well, Shako had never heard of a military drone on a mission over the Pacific, but it probably happened.

Shako gave a thumbs-up, but his thumb looked like it was wavering, just a little. Elwood grinned sympathetically. Shako hated himself.

He owed everything to Elwood and wanted to please him. And he was both jealous and envious of Jeremy, a guy who did not have to work at being impressive and who had kept his mouth shut just now.

And he wanted Jeremy to like him. He was Ted Tygart's son, after all, and there was a future in getting along with Jeremy. Furthermore, Shako had a philosophical attitude toward making enemies. He had seen how easy it was to kill people, no trouble at all, and as a result he felt that maybe one living friend was more important than many dead enemies. You could always kill someone who bothered you, even a little. But a friend had to be courted, jollied along, fed protein bars.

Shako didn't mind. He saw the big picture.

"It was a bird," said Elwood. "We hit a bird."

"Frigate bird," said Jeremy.

"Tropic bird, I bet," said Elwood.

He reached over in front of Jeremy and touched the fissures in the windscreen. The Plexiglas in front of Elwood was undamaged.

Elwood looked back at Shako again.

"I'm sorry, Mr. Quinn," he said in that respectful way.

You needed Elwood's respect. More than that—you needed him to like you. That's why Shako had exaggerated his exploits in California, said that he had used an Uzi to kill a bunch of guys in the Home Depot parking lot. It was not true, but it had been a part of his instant legend.

Elwood was an alternate father to Shako, but a dad who showed Shako how to kill and make money, an interesting alternative to real parenting. And Shako's exploits had shortly become true, when he killed an Australian couple in a blue and white yacht off Lahaina, and a couple of Americans in a catamaran off Hanalei harbor, whale watchers and tourists with too much cash on board.

There had been one other guy, a clip fired into his head off Hilo, where there had been an actual contract, with big bucks going to Shako. And it was all too easy, following Elwood's instructions, all that gun lore you heard about marksmanship and nerve just empty talk. With an Ingram submachine gun on full automatic you just let the equipment do all the work.

Shako's actual, biological dad looked like Ulysses S. Grant on the fifty-dollar bill, whiskery and hungover. His mom looked like Andrew Jackson on the twenty-dollar bill, pensive and quietly alarmed, except with lipstick and eyeliner. They had run a business that sold pea gravel and river stone, sharp-edged quarry gravel for construction, along with high quality sand and premium chicken wire.

If you had to buy fireclay or Portland cement Chuck Quinn's

Building Supply was the place, but it turned out that his parents were facing prison time for helping get rid of dead bodies on behalf of local gangs. There had not been much choice. When the street gangs of Richmond, California, said they wanted you to plop a couple of gunshot victims in the foundation of the new Taco Bell you did just that.

These days his dad was in the men's colony in Vacaville, but his mom was in a hospital for the criminally disturbed in Atascadero. Shako did not think his mother was insane—far from it. But she had gotten into a very violent fight with the public defender, furious with him for cutting such a bad deal with the prosecution.

Shako had been ordered by the court to go and live with his maternal uncle in Lihue, Kauai, in the state of Hawaii.

Uncle Andy was a man who looked like his sister, except bald. His wife looked like a Q-tip, skinny with overly bleached hair, and the two ran an auto supply for Budget and Alamo car rental agencies, ordering brake pads and timing belts from the Mainland or Japan. They put in eighteen-hour days, and when Shako went increasingly missing, they were eager to be reassured that he was staying with neighborhood families to be closer to school.

Shako liked Hawaii. He liked the pale geckos that came out at night and the way the nights were never cold. He liked the way people smiled, easy, and had all the time in the world to just stand around, not even talking. Just enjoying life. A lot of people his age skipped school, sucking strawberry-flavored shave ice and filtering back into the sugarcane fields if a cop car approached.

Shako had begun holding cash and drugs, even weapons, for older guys, because as a juvenile the law would be easier on him if he got caught. He would hang out by the abandoned sugar refinery out by Koloa and pick up whatever needed to be distributed to the tourists at the shoreline hotels, dealing with middlemen, but that ended after only a month when a rangy, red-haired guy in a white Chevy pickup told him to get in and start his new and wealthy future as a valuable member of team Tygart.

So now here he was, the aircraft gradually gaining altitude again, Jeremy laughing now that it was over, and Shako felt how great it would be to have a life like Jeremy's. Jeremy was even good at conversation, saying that an albatross was big enough to cause damage if it collided at speed, talking like a bird expert or an aircraft authority. Or both.

"Yeah, the albatross would for sure do a lot of damage," Elwood was agreeing.

And Shako thought how bad he himself was at making conversation. That was one of the things he liked about the Hawaiian fields, when the sugarcane had been burned off and plowed clean. The white-feathered cattle egrets settled in, spearing bugs with their yellow beaks, and you and your friends could just walk in the tropical breeze, nothing to say, and no need to talk.

Shako tightened the seat belt around his middle and felt

that he was the expendable member of the team, the wrestling partner who would get beaten up almost fatally so the more handsome fighter would take revenge, to everyone's delight.

Shako wanted to be the hero. He wanted to be liked. He wanted Elwood to say, "Good job, Shako." Shako wanted to maybe rescue Jeremy from danger. A shark or a stingray—pull Jeremy out of the surf at a climactic moment. Shako wanted Elwood to say what an asset Shako was, a brave man. And then Elwood would take Shako into the Tygart home with the big glass windows, a place Shako had never actually entered, and speak with Ted Tygart, a man Shako had never met in person. Elwood would say, "This is the toughest guy I ever hired."

So Shako began to pull together phrases he could use later on. But it was not easy. What could he say? Right now Elwood was offering a typical Elwood remark: "Tropic birds circle for altitude, Jeremy, and maintain it for hours without actually moving their wings."

You know, Jeremy, Shako could say, the big problem with guns is blowback, bits of the guy getting all over you.

No one wanted to hear that. So Shako would keep quiet. If he spoke at all, death would come out, like in the talk bubble over a cartoon character's head. Names and last words, like how the Australian woman begged for her life, in that tweaked accent, *please, we'll give you anything*.

And shooting them wasn't even fun, no more than using a weed whacker on the ti plants behind his uncle's house.

Shako knew his world. He had seen *Friday Night*

SmackDown Live when it broadcast out of Oakland. He had the autographs of nineteen professional wrestlers from the convention in Sacramento, signed in black Magic Marker, beautiful swirling names with underlines and exclamation points. A professional wrestler was a complete package, like Elwood, knowing how to shake hands and say *thanks for being here, my man*, even to a kid.

Shako knew he would end up dead. Just like Mo Millimeter, the guy who shot up the Hilton in Waikiki and who lived on through the Web, graffiti, and T-shirts. Just like suicide bombers and famous killer rap artists. Being dead was just the price. You were dead, but you were big.

Shako pulled out his phone right there in the airplane and watched a video of himself changing expressions, no smile, small smile, and the video of him loading the Ingram, then breaking the weapon down. Shako liked the way he looked. He liked the picture of him with green and gray camouflage grease Elwood had bought him, real Marine Corps face goop. He was a one-man strike force.

"THE CRACKS ARE ALL ON THE SURFACE, see?" said Elwood. "No airflow comes through."

"So this isn't an emergency?" Jeremy was asking.

"Not even close, Jeremy. Not even a serious annoyance."

Elwood was happy but even when he wasn't he kept a smile stuck onto his face, welcome and virile, the kind of smile that attracted young men to adventure and women to a night of muscular romance from time to time. His one true love, Zeta, used to say he had the best smile in the world. She had been a caring, considerate woman he almost never let enter his mind.

"Just so I know," said Jeremy, "give me an example of an emergency."

"Shako's machine gun going off by accident, cutting me in two," said Elwood, "and you having to fly back to Kauai all by yourself. That would be an emergency."

"That would be terrible, Elwood!"

"What, me getting killed?"

"I would hate that."

Elwood was touched. Jeremy was an amiable young man. More than that—a decent person.

Mr. Tygart had insisted that Jeremy take this trip, a search and rescue mission, but Tygart had expected to find Kyle alive after overstating reports of his own demise, Kyle a known joker and a youthful exaggerator of his own plight. But this hunt was going on too long, and Elwood knew there was going to be more trouble than Mr. Tygart had anticipated.

Plus, Tygart had not authorized the addition of Shako to the trip. But Elwood was finished personally killing people or animals—he had long ago outgrown the practice, and he thought of Shako as a pair of gloves, non-latex laboratory gloves. Plus, if a dead body had to be handled, Elwood's philosophy was: let younger men do it.

Elwood gave a glance into the back. Shako was either asleep or gone into lizard-mode, his cell phone in his hand, watching a video. A good killer can do that. You could plug them into an MP3 and tell them to wait. They would sit for hours, stand up and kill a guy, and then sit for another ten hours, never a complaint.

"But the Ingram is here in front, in one of these bags, right?" Jeremy was asking.

"Sure," said Elwood. "Safe and snug."

"I think I could manage, Elwood," Jeremy added. "I could pilot the plane back to Nawiliwili, if I had to."

"Sure, I know you would manage, no problem," said Elwood. "You've been a good learner."

Elwood loved teaching young people—how to keep the aircraft engines from icing up, how to program the in-flight computer, and in the case of someone like Shako, how to bring the target down and how to finish them.

You had to be able to finish.

Elwood used to pilot a relic DC3 up from Sinaloa, Mexico, flying at night, easing it down on an airstrip marked by flashlights just across the border. He liked having the Arizona landscape all around, and every predawn that he stepped out into the desert air and watched the furtive crew unload marijuana in plastic sacks, he would pace and flex his arms and legs, eager for the return flight.

He had met Ted Tygart at the yacht club at Hanalei Bay, Kauai's glamour-set enjoying the semitropical night, and Elwood between jobs. The West Coast was a free-for-all in recent years, tunnels under the California/Mexico border taking the place of night flights, and Elwood wanted to keep his piloting skills intact.

Hawaii's economy had collapsed, and a few of the big hotels were becoming places where money was laundered, the cocktail lounges and weight rooms fronts for illegal sources of cash. Elwood ferried money by air from Lahaina to Hilo, and from Kona to Hana, an expert at water landings and loving his work.

Ted Tygart heard of this rangy, red-haired cowboy who took guns and drugs by air from one hidden bay to another throughout the islands, and when Elwood had a Heineken with Tygart in his wonderland near Poipu Beach, Elwood knew he had found his dream employer, a man who could bribe law enforcement and pay off his competition, everybody happy.

Elwood loved to go places and he loved to come back. Take the recent dive, for example, a big frigate bird smacking them hard. Sure, he had been personally surprised, but they had not been in any serious danger. Much of the dive had been just to get them down below the altitude of other large birds, the seafowl circling high and heading north and west to get away from the coming bad weather.

"Jeremy," Elwood said now, "get on the radio again and see if you can't get *Witch Grass*."

Jeremy did as he was told. Elwood liked to be obeyed, and having the boss's son with him gave him both a feeling of responsibility and a sense of the trust Ted Tygart felt.

"Still no answer," Jeremy reported.

"That is a distressed vessel somewhere down there, Jeremy," chided Elwood. "Distressed and lost. You keep trying to raise them. You wanted to know a good example of an emergency. Being lost at sea is a good example."

Of the two missing guys, Kyle Molline was a likable individual, just a little older than Jeremy, learning to play the guitar, an easygoing type in baggy shorts who also did whatever Elwood told him to do. Paul Aiken was thin, bald, and eager to please, *Mr. Elwood, sir, can I get you another beer?* He had one steel tooth, the handiwork of a dentist in Halawa Correctional Facility on the island of Oahu. Elwood did not like Paul.

But then Elwood liked Shako. And when it was all done, Elwood would have to see that Shako met an early demise. Not on this flight, most likely. But within the next month or two, while Shako went target shooting on the Na Pali cliffs or while he was watching cage fighting on Blu-ray at Elwood's condo, some means would be found to lose the young man, and put him in a bait cooler and feed his body to the sea life off Barking Sands, the empty, hardscrabble beach on the western edge of Kauai.

There was no choice, Elwood told himself with an air of inner peace. It was all a matter of finishing the job. And behind Shako there was a long line of young men hanging out in video arcades and Pizza Huts, thirteen- and fourteen-year-olds who would love to learn how to handle a submachine gun, blow up a jacaranda or feral chicken out behind Mount Nonou, where no cops ever cruised.

"When I first started flying," said Elwood, "you could see huge schools of albacore in the Pacific, shining limbs of light, all the way toward the horizon."

He turned as he said this, speaking to Shako. And then he stopped himself. Why was he talking to Shako? The young man probably didn't know what an albacore was.

"Tuna fish," said Shako, with his thin lips and his sunglasses.

He said *tuna fish* like Elwood had as a kid. Tuna fish sandwiches with pickle relish and lots of mayonnaise had been his favorite lunch. He would come home from Pacifica High School, where he lived just south of San Francisco, and his mother would have one waiting for him on a paper plate.

She'd be off to business school, studying all the different ways to subtract money. It was all subtraction, Elwood thought, ever since his mother died of breast cancer and his dad had suffered a stroke at the age of forty-four, outside the Daly City Post Office, where he was in the process of being arrested by USPS inspectors for mail fraud.

"You could see the albacore chasing away sharks," said Elwood. "Strength in numbers."

He looked back at Shako and the kid gave him what had to be a smile. A further tightening of the lips, a pucker of one cheek.

Elwood couldn't help himself—he liked Shako more and more. It was going to be a sad day when he had the young man killed.

THE YACHT WAS INCREASINGLY ALIVE, surging through the seas. Martin sat with his uncle, getting out the map.

The shelves of the yacht were full of books about seabirds and shipwrecks, submarine kills and boat design. At one end of the shelves, held snugly in place by a horizontal rod, was a healthy collection of well-thumbed paperbacks, but even they had a nautical flavor: novels by Patrick O'Brian and translations of Greek myths, the gods competing with each other in crushing mariners.

Leonard had studied law and passed the bar exam, but had never set foot in a courtroom. He had specialized in land development and had prospered. But the construction of malls and huge exurban homes had been in a severe nosedive in recent years.

Leonard's father, Martin's grandfather, was Tyler Burgess, an assistant prop manager for Paramount, specializing in everything from derringers to bazookas. Tyler Burgess endured an on-again, off-again career, as movie fashions vacillated from crime to war to sci-fi and back again. He had urged his two sons to find steadier employment.

Now Leonard had a plastic map of the Pacific spread out in front of him. It was about the size of a large board game, and he used a black marker to show their new position, using the GPS unit he kept clipped to his belt.

The distance from San Francisco to Hawaii was about two thousand four hundred land miles, and if they managed a speed of ten miles per hour, twenty-four hours a day, they could in theory make the distance in ten days. But weather, wind, and currents were unpredictable, and making way generally required more caution. Most voyages to the islands took the better part of a month, and this crossing was likely to be no exception.

Martin had a cabin on the starboard side, not far from Leonard and Claudette's master compartment. Susannah occupied a cabin on the port side, taking her pick of several vacancies. Axel had a cabin well forward on the same side, not far from the galley.

Athena's Secret was a sixty-foot wooden-hulled yacht with every comfort—two hot showers, private sleeping facilities, and air-conditioning. She was nearly twenty feet across at the widest point, and she had tanks that held four tons of fuel and a similar quantity of fresh water.

The vessel boasted two Sitka spruce masts and auxiliary power consisting of twin four-hundred-horsepower Caterpillar engines. She was outfitted with a Raytheon automatic pilot, but someone was expected to be at the helm around the clock.

Leonard had ordered the yacht built by a boatyard in

Bodega Bay, on California's Mendocino coast, years before, when he was just out of law school and had some family money to go with his grand prospects. Bill Ingbord, the legendary Danish shipwright, had designed her, laid her keel, and had seen her through every stage of construction. Leonard had christened the vessel *Athena's Secret*, and he enjoyed giving the inside story regarding her name.

In Greek legend, a wandering adventurer named Tiresias was struck blind by Athena, the goddess of wisdom, because he accidentally saw her naked as she bathed in a stream. She regretted her rash punishment, but she could not undo her curse. So she gave Tiresias the gift of prophecy, and he became a renowned seer.

Leonard enjoyed explaining that the secret of Athena was not only her nakedness—which a mortal dare not look upon—but her power and willingness to compensate for her own mistakes. Recompense was one of the fundamentals of law, Leonard liked to say, and this made her name especially sweet to an aspiring lawyer.

But Martin knew that there was another explanation for her name: Leonard was superstitious.

Because there was another fascinating detail regarding *Athena's Secret*. Just as struggling mountaineers sometimes felt themselves in the presence of an unknown companion, and lovers sometimes sensed an unknown third party in the room, so Leonard had more than once told of feeling that when he was alone on the vessel he was not really alone. He told this to everyone—Axel, Martin, and even the harbormaster of the marina in San Francisco, but only Martin understood that his uncle was not joking or striking a colorful pose.

Leonard sometimes said that when he had to make a difficult decision he asked the boat for her advice and listened carefully.

Open-minded but gently skeptical, Martin had never had such a dialogue with the yacht himself.

"Where are we?" he asked.

"Our location," said Leonard, "is latitude 26 degrees, 16.4 minutes north, longitude 143 degrees, 56.0 minutes west. Bearing south-southwest."

"Are you sure about all that?" asked Martin jokingly.

There could be no doubt. No one with decent equipment was ever really lost.

"You aren't worried, are you?" asked Leonard.

Martin said, "A little."

"We're going right into the low pressure system, Martin," said Leonard. "Head on. We have no choice, really."

"Why is that?" Martin knew he was expected to ask.

"If we flee the storm," said Leonard, "we'll get hit by what they call a following sea. Waves will batter our stern and we'll wallow. If we travel sideways to the weather, we'll struggle, too, and maybe turn over. It happens. Heading right into it is the only way. Besides, we don't want to back down from a challenge, do we?"

"But about that other thing," Martin began.

"What thing?" asked Leonard, although Martin had the feeling he already knew.

He did not like to press his uncle, but the subject had to be brought up.

"How are we going to defend ourselves?" Martin asked.

Leonard smiled. "I'll take care of you."

Maybe, thought Martin.

But maybe not. Seaplanes often worked with a surface vessel in tandem. Maritime violence was on the news all the time, innocent families held hostage, raped, killed.

THE DAY BEFORE EASTER, three months earlier, Martin had been witness to an upsetting incident.

He had been waiting for a Bay Area Rapid Transit train to San Francisco, on his way to see a film at the Imax Theater at Yerba Buena Center. The movie was *These Are Pearls*, a movie about coral reefs and the future of the oceans. Tom Yinn, his friend from calculus, was going to meet him there, and they would have a turkey sandwich at Lefty O'Doul's afterward.

But Martin never saw the movie.

Instead, someone jumped off the platform of the Lake Merritt Station, in front of an oncoming train. The man had worn a blue-striped, short-sleeved dress shirt, light blue pants, and a pair of Ecco dress shoes with all-terrain soles.

Martin had a vivid recollection of the clothing, because within an instant the man had been reduced to his clothes as the steel wheels of the six-car train rolled over him, and the man's body rolled with it. The blue pant legs went boneless and scarlet as they spun forward on the rails, along with the shrieking, slowly halting wheels.

The police had been considerate, but in an official,

checklist way. *Show us again where he was standing, please.* At last, a BART cop had recognized how shaken Martin was and drove him home.

Shaken did not begin to describe his feelings.

Weeks after the incident, Martin forced himself to read news accounts on the Web. The man had been a composer, and the San Francisco Symphony had been set to perform the world premiere of the artist's newest work. What fault lines of the composer's psyche had worked to destroy him Martin could not guess. But he downloaded some of the artist's work. They were stately, abstract symphonic pieces that were beyond Martin's ability to judge, but they certainly gave no hint of their creator's ultimate despair and destruction.

His parents had met with Dr. Metz, the family physician, and the doctor had recommended a summer break, far from Oakland and full of sky and sun. Dad had known exactly what sort of trip would do the job. He had made a phone call, and now here Martin was, in the middle of the Pacific and, when you considered the voyage from every angle, really enjoying himself.

Every morning after breakfast on the yacht, Martin had a routine. He did an inventory of what needed to be repaired. This morning that meant that the latch on the door from the cabin would need to be fixed—the door was supposed to open from the outside in, which meant that seas and wind tended to force it shut. But now it was swinging both ways, a quirk it had acquired overnight. Martin made a mental note to patch up the fastening after the storm had passed, but the door had never fastened securely, and, Martin suspected, never would.

In addition to shipboard chores such as rubbing tung oil on teakwood and Brasso on all the metal frames and fittings, he always looked forward to a daily phone call to his parents, a call that was possible because of the small satellite transmitter on the mast.

This morning was no exception.

But just before he made this call he ran various rehearsals through his mind.

Remember, Dad, he wanted to ask, how Leonard used to race freight trains in his vintage MG, until you told him he was frightening everyone who loved him? Remember how he shot the Tuolumne River white water every year in a kayak, until he hit a bridge piling and nearly drowned? You got him to quit.

Martin was on deck, as far out of earshot from anyone as he could get, near the prow, and before he made the call, he enjoyed his feeling of solitude—a rare experience at sea.

A jellyfish slipped along on the ocean surface as he held the phone to his ear, the floating creature little more than a lovely, nearly transparent nova on the water. Two time zones ahead of California, he caught them while Dad was putting on his tennis shoes, heading out for an early morning match with his more athletic friends.

Dad was not a very good tennis player—he tended to fight

the ball back across the net with too much gusto, and his serves were overpowered and wild. But people liked to play the game with him. He shouted when he missed, and he shouted when he won, and he was a cheerful loser. Martin had never yearned to be with his father more than he did right then.

The digital connection was good, but almost too good, amplifying his dad's breathing as plainly as his cheerful "God, we miss you, Marty."

Martin's father was a produce department manager, organic California vegetables his specialty. Martin's mother, Beatrice, was a sensitive, slightly overweight woman, given to sulks if a manager reminded her to sign in on the right line on the time sheet. After a series of jobs at a florist and at a party supply store, she had settled on working from home, designing greeting cards, rag-paper prints that looked like Japanese woodcuts.

She had good years and bad years financially, loading the family van with inventory and driving to crafts fairs and street festivals. In recent years, an improved Web site had helped her business, and now she had turned the family's North Oakland garage into an office/warehouse, stacks of shipping envelopes and art paper in every corner.

Dad did sound a lot like his younger brother, Leonard, on the phone now, but less dramatic. Dad's methodical husbandry came through in the way he named the places he was walking through, looking for his wife—not in the sewing room, not in the living room—until he found her in the garage, stapling envelopes.

She got on her own phone, and then her breath was added to the chorus of breathing sounds. The computer that processed this call must not have been able to tell the difference between breathing and talking, and the three of them sounded like humpback whales on the surface after an hour in the deep.

"You use a lot of that sunblock, Martin," she said, "and stick plenty of that zinc paste on your nose."

Mom was like that, speaking out of a maternal codebook, a cipher that translated love into a grim classification of increasingly fraught concerns—skin cancer, broken bones, hypothermia, death.

The only way to respond to the code was to say that you were in truth being careful. He could hear her working, holding the phone to her ear by cocking her head to one side. She stapled bags shut as she talked, the stapler making a pleasant *ka-chunk* sound.

In answer to how things were going, Martin replied, as always, with that casually reassuring "Things are good," but now as he heard the words, what he wanted to ask was *Have you seen the weather map this morning?*

His dad answered the question before he had to, because he had in fact seen the weather chart on the Web, and he said that it did look like some serious weather.

Serious weather. The word *serious* was a significant part of his dad's vocabulary. A garden could be seriously good-looking, and an athlete possess a serious throwing arm.

His dad added, after a split-second hesitation, "But I know that Leonard will sail away from trouble."

Martin thought about this.

"Uncle Leonard's eager to dive right into the storm," said Martin after a pause. He made this remark sound offhand.

"Eager?" asked Dad thoughtfully, as though Leonard's eagerness was not always a characteristic to be admired or relied on.

"Enthusiastic, maybe," said Martin.

"Well," said Beatrice, "I'm sure he knows what he's doing." She had stopped stapling.

Perhaps Martin expected a blanket dismissal of his worries, but what he got was strangely unsettling, even as it showed his dad's faith in him.

"Use your head, Martin," Dad said.

His father hesitated to say more. Martin could sense his father's conscience working through family politics, his knowledge of his brother's history, and his desire not to unduly alarm either his wife or Martin.

"You go right ahead," said Dad, "and give Leonard hell if it looks like he's about to get you all drowned."

THEIR AIRSPEED was one hundred and ninety-eight miles per hour, about as fast as the de Havilland could go. The heading indicator showed that they were traveling east-northeast, outrunning the storm, which the aviation weather radio channel had defined as a "very well-formed depression heading in a northerly direction."

Jeremy imagined the storm as a creature shaped like a timber saw, a wheel with ragged blades. You could see it on the radar screen, hovering over *Witch Grass*, swallowing the pulsing zit of light, coming right after Jeremy.

Jeremy handled the stick himself, piloting the plane. It was not actually a stick so much as the portion of a wheel, padded and shaped like half a Frisbee.

"Watch the artificial horizon," said Elwood, leaning forward to tap the attitude indicator.

The display showed whether the aircraft was level from side to side and whether the nose was angling too high or too low. They were heading slightly downward, and Jeremy eased the nose up until the plane was level again, and then overcompensated. The engine changed its timbre, taking on a lower note, the machinery somehow recognizing that a new pilot was in command.

As Elwood had reached out to touch the cockpit display, Jeremy had once again noticed the scar on his right hand. Someone had bitten Elwood years ago, between his thumb and forefinger. Maybe a man, maybe a dog.

"Is it true," Jeremy asked, "that you tried to kill Laser when he was a pup?"

"I tried to drown him," said Elwood smoothly, as though this was a perfectly reasonable answer.

"Why?"

"He chewed up a new pair of Corcoran combat boots," said Elwood, "and Kyle wouldn't shoot him like I wanted, just offered to buy me a new pair. Which he did—these are the ones he bought me."

"So it all worked out."

"Not really. I took the dog out to the Hanalei River in a garbage bag and would have thrown him in but Kyle stopped me. The dog hates me ever since. He got big and ugly, but he didn't change toward me."

"I'd hate you, too," said Jeremy.

Elwood gave him a you-can't-please-everyone smile. "I have to work at it," said Elwood.

"At what?" asked Jeremy.

"At being a human baseball bat," said Elwood, rubbing his eyes and blinking. "I have to keep inventing ways to impress your dad, making sure the dealers don't cheat him, rejecting counterfeit bills and phony artifacts, picking up heavy stuff and loading it myself."

"Who taught you to do all this?" asked Jeremy.

Picking up heavy stuff was probably a euphemism for murder.

Elwood dug into his hip pocket and brought out his wallet, a thin, black leather fold. He slipped out a small photo and showed it to Jeremy without giving it to him. A young woman in a halter top smiled at the camera, one hand up to keep the sun off her face. She looked way too young for Elwood, the kind of person you see with other young women, talking and laughing. The shadows of her fingers fell across her forehead. The photo was slightly tattered and the colors had grown dim.

Elwood glanced into the back. Shako was awake after all, leaning forward so he could hear.

Elwood gave Shako the photo for a moment.

"She was my fiancée, twenty years ago," said Elwood. "Her name was Zeta Durant."

"She looks like a very nice person," said Jeremy.

Shako gave the photo back and stayed as he was, leaning forward, so he could hear what Elwood was saying.

"She worked at the airstrip where I used to have a job," Elwood continued. "She ran the office, payroll, accounts. I fueled Cessnas and kept the padlock on the gate."

Jeremy was surprised. "You had a regular job?"

"They never caught the guy who killed her in Fremont, California," Elwood continued, "the day before Halloween. She was walking home on payday, got mugged, fell and fractured her skull, and I hunted down bad guys for a long time after that. The wrong bad guys, but they were better than nothing."

And dogs had gotten to her body, Elwood did not want to add. No need to upset Jeremy with the heartbreaking details. But the reports in the news said that a feral pack had meant her remains could not be identified for a week after her bones were in the coroner's fridge.

"That's terrible," said Jeremy, meaning more than he could say.

Elwood put the picture back into his wallet. "I realized I would make a better bad guy than every single one of the criminals I snuffed, so here I am."

The main fuel supply was fourth-fifths empty. Jeremy could feel how much lighter the aircraft was, nearly one hundred and fifty gallons more buoyant. The auxiliary tank held a comparable amount, and Jeremy tried to calculate how much search time they had before they had to head back to Kauai.

The aircraft leaped and shuddered, the wings banking without any command on Jeremy's part. He kept his feet on the rudder pedals and eased the aircraft back to horizontal flight.

Not bad, thought Jeremy. I'm not doing that badly.

Elwood was on the radio, his singsong, laid-back radio voice the stuff of aviation cliché. "*Witch Grass*, this is *Red Bird*, do you copy?"

The airplane was hitting turbulence, outlying eddies of air that were invisible and smacked the aircraft hard. Very hard—

the cockpit jostled and shook, and Jeremy's teeth snapped together.

All of this would have been fun, except that there was nothing sporting about it from where Jeremy was sitting, his eyes on the altimeter, a digital device with numbers that kept changing, adding and subtracting feet as the invisible torrents in the atmosphere grabbed at the aircraft.

AXEL OWEN STOOD at the helm, and as he gripped the spokes of the wooden wheel and felt the vessel respond, he knew that this, exactly this, was what he was made to do.

Axel did not think that he was a very complicated guy. He was simple the way a thumb is simple. He loved the yacht and he was in love with Susannah.

He loved *Athena's Secret* because never, in his entire life, had he ever awakened in a place that was designed to be beautiful. And every cleat and wale on this yacht had been conceived and crafted to be a thing of loveliness.

This made the yacht unique in his experience. Axel had lived, at various times in his life, in apartments in Oakland, one- and two-bedroom duplexes with cockroaches like freeway traffic and rats like railroad cars, hurrying nonstop. His widowed mother had paid rent for illegal basement crannies with aluminum foil over naked lath and plaster, places where you were happy to have a mouse race his four scampering paws across the kitchen floor—at least it was company.

So he loved the yacht and would mentally say it was four stars.

His budding relationship with Susannah, however, could not be rated so highly. He was attracted to her because she was unlike any young woman he had ever known. He had played liar's dice with the women in the bars along San Pablo Avenue, places where it was illegal for an eighteen-year-old to sit and order beer, but Axel had always looked older than he was. Susannah was not like them.

Right then Martin climbed out on deck, looking fit and healthy and just that much of a rival.

"Is your uncle serious about gaffing that shark?" asked Axel.

Martin smiled. Martin was what everyone would call a nice guy, and Axel knew that he himself was not. But Martin was not only nice. He was other things, too. Martin was knowing and uncompetitive, as though life had already held a speed trial and Martin had won.

"You never know with Uncle Leonard," said Martin.

"Well, if you want the job done," said Axel, "just tell Mr. Burgess to say the word."

Martin just laughed. Not an all-out laugh, but a brainy chuckle.

"I mean it," said Axel.

"Sure you do," said Martin.

Martin was letting Axel know that he got the fact that Axel would love to show off, clubbing a sea predator to death. It was all about Susannah. But it was hard to get Susannah's attention, Axel knew too well.

She was one of those people completely wired up to their

own nervous systems. Even now she was probably in her cabin, tapping her impression of the voyage into her computer. All about her feelings, and birds. No mention of me at all, probably, Axel thought.

As if that weren't bad enough, Axel was losing money in a big way, playing online Texas hold 'em right here on the yacht every night. He had an account at GamblingPlanet, gaming 24/7. He had already lost more than he would make on this voyage, and Leonard was a generous employer.

Plus, he had to eat Leonard's food, and the man could cook well enough to please his own family, but Axel had been a cook's mate on a freighter from Oakland to Vancouver. This had been one week after his sixteenth birthday, a fresh high school dropout working for a retired navy cook with no teeth and a glass eye, a man who could serve osso buco or bananas Foster right out of his cramped, neat little galley.

Axel had learned how to make mushrooms in white wine and Boeuf à la Catalane, and all the sauces from béchamel to curry, and the men on the *Brazos IV* loved it, scarfed it right up, a crew you'd think would be about equal to pizza.

He had learned how to tie a granny knot and a timber hitch and a dozen other knots, and he had learned how to act sober when he was drunk, returning to Oakland with a case of crab lice and a paycheck from DaCaspar Shipping. He found work steadily after that, too young to be legal but cheap as a result. He had worked up and down the Sacramento River on dredging barges, and troll and salmon fishing trips, crewing outside the Golden Gate with rich people, which was how he had met Mr. and Mrs. Burgess. He liked the Burgesses. He really did.

But even now he had to say, "What have you ever had to fight for, Martin?"

He knew he was acting like a macho jerk, but the challenge was in him and it had to come out somehow. Martin was destined to be a scientist or a TV personality and Axel could see himself standing at the helm of someone else's yacht for decades, until he was toothless and had a glass eye himself. Two glass eyes, probably. It rankled.

"What have I fought for?" said Martin. "Oh, I don't know. I think maybe fighting is overrated."

He was not even troubled by the question, he was so unintimidated and so completely commonsensical. Axel recalled, a little too late, that Martin had witnessed a regrettable event on a BART platform, and maybe talking about combat was not a friendly course to take. Axel also recognized that although he had once nearly stomped a rat to death on Fruitvale Avenue, the rat had escaped—rats turned out to be acrobatic as well as tough. Axel was not really any more dangerous than the next person, although he would like to be thought so.

"How about you?" Martin went on to ask. "I bet you've been a terror up and down the West Coast."

Joking about it, thought Alex. Rich people, they'd laugh about anything.

Axel's late father, Billy Owen, had been a gambler, playing

pai gow card clubs all night and Golden Gate Fields horse racing all afternoon, and making money at it, too. His friends in Vegas had called him "Billy Owe 'em." This had been a humorous name, rather than accurate—he had actually lived debt-free and had filed a tax return every year as a professional gambler.

His mom, Dixie Owen, played along, too, and successfully, until Billy dropped dead from heart failure holding a winning Trifecta ticket on California Derby Day. Dixie cashed in the ticket, married a man from El Centro who sold guns from the trunk of his vintage Trans Am. The man was named Sol Capo, and he was a good hand at restoring old weapons. Axel had liked Sol, and the experience of seeing how he made a living— showing guys how to blow targets to confetti with military surplus on full auto. But basically Mom had moved out of Axel's young life.

Axel decided to change the subject just as Martin was powering up his laptop and getting another good look at the weather map, shielding the computer from the salt spray. Another thing Axel had noticed about people with money: they were always checking their phones and their computers, staying connected.

"What do you hear from Susannah, Martin?" Axel hated the way he sounded, so needful. He had brought up the subject before, and Martin had usually offered his kindly silent laugh.

Martin said now, "I have to tell you, Axel, that I don't think she is really that crazy about you."

His tone was sympathetic, reluctant. This was a man-to-man, gentle way of saying: give up on her. Martin was the sort of person who prefaced bad news with *I'm sorry, but*.

This hurt Axel's feelings. He would have to be tough—stoical. Axel had always prided himself on keeping his mouth shut and using few words. If Axel had bad news he would just say it. This was a good policy. Why was he talking so much this morning?

The sea was choppy, turning to swells. The coming storm made him nervous.

"Your uncle," he said, "is out on the prow, doing something. I'm worried."

This got Martin's attention.

The clouds had piled up to the west, layers of them. A piece of something swept past in the rough water, a slab of shipping container—a floating razor to a wooden hull.

At times the propellers were forced out of the water, and they made a determined whining noise until the yacht dropped back down into the sea. To be on deck was to be wet, and Axel and Martin had both donned bright yellow waterproof jackets and high black boots. Even so, salt water stung their eyes and lips.

Axel didn't bother to say anything more, just gazed out from the helm, keeping them as steady as possible at ten knots per hour, fast enough that seas crashed into and over the yacht, soaking every inch of rigging and making the scuppers overflow.

And the yacht was laboring. There was something slowing her, forcing her back. Moment by moment she was less nimble, less seaworthy. There was the faintest sensation of trouble communicated through the deck underfoot.

"You better go forward, Martin," said Axel, "and see what's wrong."

MARTIN MADE HIS WAY along the yacht, clinging to the rail outside the cabins, heading toward the prow.

The sun was still bright, but the clouds ahead of them looked like a gigantic chunk of nighttime, ripped out and stuck against the blue.

"Don't come out here," Leonard called into the wind. "Martin, it's not safe."

A great wad of fishing net had plowed into the prow, looking like a giant, diaphanous amoeba that spun out tendrils. Leonard was grabbing at it, hauling at it, trying to free the yacht from the seaborne mess. Martin joined in the great effort, seizing the netting and trying to drag it to starboard.

The netting, which had floated in a tangled hairball of filament and sea slime all the way from Malaysia, as far as Martin could tell, was like a living thing determined to make the vessel its new purchase on life.

Leonard was struggling to stay where he was, hanging on to the rail along the ship's prow with his bright yellow waterproof gloves, the sea washing over him. He was wearing one of the waterproof jackets, too, and with the hood folded back it gave him a weather-soaked, heroic appearance.

Martin could see the aspiring football player in his uncle now, not good enough to be a starter but showing up for practice every day. He also looked a little crazy, as though if the water pounded him hard enough it might wash him off and drown him and he wouldn't mind.

The two of them attacked the great bolus of fishing filament once again, and this time they made progress. Part of the netting tore and released its grip on the prow. The yacht was still tangled, but the fight was no longer hopeless.

A wave broke across the prow, and Leonard had to get a fresh grip to keep from being swept away.

"What would the boat tell you to do?" asked Martin. "If she spoke to you—what would she say?"

"What?" called Leonard, either not understanding Martin's question, with the seas crashing, or not wanting to.

"What would she tell you?"

"I don't know," said Leonard, blinking against the salt water that came from all directions.

"Ask her," called Martin against the shriek of the wind.

Leonard gave a nod and squinted, readying his resolve for a serious inquiry. But what he said surprised Martin. "I never really believed all that, Martin. About talking to the spirit of the boat. I made that all up."

Martin was relieved to hear that Leonard was not a superstitious nut, but he was a little disappointed, too. Some small part of him had wanted to believe in such things.

Leonard saw his nephew's distress.

"I could ask her anyway," he suggested.

Martin gave a nod, his weatherproof gear creaking like plastic armor.

"What should I do?" called Leonard into the gale. "*Athena*, tell me how to act with everything in shreds, all the air and all the water, and my life with it."

It had seemed like a wry joke at first, but now it was all too serious. His uncle was a little unhinged after all, Martin saw. Maybe Leonard was hoping a karate chop of water would knock him off the yacht and Claudette and Susannah could thrive on the proceeds of his life insurance policy.

His uncle cocked his head, and he looked like a man listening to a faint, nearly indistinct signal.

"Ship of mine," he cried now, "beautiful vessel—what should I do?"

He held his head at another angle, and for an instant Martin had the uncanny sense that Leonard was listening to a communication meant only for his ears. Martin also had the impression that Leonard was not inviting simple advice about his own safety.

Maybe Leonard felt dread, too.

And he needed to know what would happen.

At that moment an enormous wave, laced with foam and simmering, heaved against the prow, and Leonard was nearly washed away. Martin seized his uncle, gripped him by the arm, his own glove squeaking against Leonard's nylon sleeve. He got a firm hold and pulled his uncle to his feet.

"Be careful," gasped Leonard, "of my back."

As they tried to make their way to the stern, the two of them had to stop more than once and hang on to the main cabin rail. When they had almost returned to relative safety, another unexpected swell struck even harder.

The yacht gave a heave, and without warning Leonard slipped, tried to find a handhold, and failed. He cried out for help. Martin grabbed him again, just in time. Leonard careened off the edge of the vessel, and Martin barely kept a grip on his uncle's hand.

Leonard hung suspended in the wind, kept from the water only by Martin's grasp, yellow glove to yellow glove. But Leonard's glove was too big, the wrong fit, and he was slowly but inexorably slipping free.

MARTIN HELD ON TO LEONARD'S ARM, to find, to his horror, that his uncle's body was suspended in midair, crashing heavily into the side of the vessel as the heavy seas increased. Leonard was calling out, something wordless and tormented.

Martin pulled hard, hauling Leonard back onto the yacht and handling him desperately, at last hurling him onto the deck beside the helm.

The rain began in earnest as Leonard lay there, even in his anguish trying to make some sort of quip. This precipitation was heavy, straight-down water. The downpour was warm as rain went, and yet it was so heavy that Martin shivered inside his waterproof jacket. One of his boots, with its top exposed beyond the skirt of his yellow jacket, was full of water in an instant.

The vessel was heaving. The helm was only a few strides away, but Martin could not see it.

"I'm hurt," said Leonard, as though this did not happen to be obvious.

Claudette hurried from the cabin, staggering with the motion of the vessel, and knelt beside him.

"Martin saved my life!" said Leonard.

Claudette touched only the rain-lanced air over his body, afraid to cause him more pain.

"How did this happen?" she asked.

"A bunch of fishing net," laughed Leonard, although his laugh sounded more like a wheeze. "A wad of filament about the size of Oakland."

Susannah was at Martin's side, gazing down at her father. She sighed, shaking her head.

"Not only is Dad hurt," she said, forgetting or deliberately choosing not to call him Leonard, "the galley just exploded."

Axel remained at the helm as Martin and Susannah carried Leonard into the cabin he shared with his wife.

Leonard was a stout man, but not very tall, and yet he felt much heavier than Martin would have thought possible. "I'm OK, perfectly all right," Leonard sang out. "No, don't stop, keep going."

They stretched him out in the bunk, surrounded by his books, histories of ancient Greece and paperbacks about sailing, book jackets featuring racing yachts and sunset-gilded sails.

"I just need to rest for a little while," said Leonard.

"What medication do we have?" asked Susannah.

"We have a terrific first aid kit," said Leonard. "From the maritime supply in Alameda, and Claudette got Dr. Tang across the street to write us some prescriptions."

"Morphine," said Claudette.

"Too strong," said Leonard. "I don't want to be plowed under."

"Be plowed under, Leonard," said Susannah, with more than a trace of kindness. "You need it."

"No, a captain has to be sharp," said Leonard. "You'll be sailing in circles without me."

"We have some codeine," said Claudette.

"Hey, codeine," said Leonard. "Always works for me."

"I'll sit here with you," said Claudette, giving him several white pills, which he chewed up like they were mints. "You'll be all right."

Martin knew that Claudette was lying, too. They were confronted with a serious injury, and Martin did not know what they could do. And he was touched by the loving concern in Claudette's voice.

"Oh, don't worry," said Leonard. "Don't stand there looking so stricken. Good work, Martin. I am the luckiest skipper in the world."

SUSANNAH LEFT HER PARENTS' CABIN, but Martin lingered, sure that a lurch of the vessel would toss Leonard from his bunk.

Susannah called to him, her voice nearly obscured by the sound of the storm.

The galley door was open. The roar of rain was all around, seeming, even from below the hull, a three-dimensional rush of noise.

The galley was a mess.

"It's my fault," said Martin.

"Martin, Dad would have drowned if not for you."

"I should have been more careful."

"Martin, look at me," she insisted. "You are not to blame. You saved his life."

He knelt and picked up a package of Birds Eye frozen peas, *Perfectly steams in the bag!*

"You don't have to help me with all this, Martin," said Susannah. "I can manage."

"So it didn't literally explode," he said.

She gave a wry smile. "An explosion would have been better."

She knelt with him on the galley floor. Containers of

condensed milk and packaged soups were scattered all over the tiny kitchen, tossed to and fro by the storm. Pots were kept in place on the shelves by railings, but food seemed to have a life of its own.

"Did you hear about that fight Leonard tried to break up," she asked, "out by Pier 39?"

Martin thought it was strange, calling your parents by their first names. But it was dynamic, too, implying an equality between parents and child.

"He tried to keep the peace, from what I heard."

"He got into a fight with two drunk guys, and anyone could have told him to mind his own business."

"Was he hurt?

"Sprained his back, of course. I hate to see Leonard suffer, Martin." Her voice was thick with feeling for a moment. "But usually, I have to point out that it's his own fault."

"That's kind of amazing, though," said Martin. "My uncle trying to stop a fight."

"Being foolish is amazing?" asked Susannah.

He laughed, the patented Martin quiet laugh—soundless, really.

Frozen steaks had escaped from the freezer, and the sight of a pink, hairless body part skittering into the saloon made Martin feel that never again would he eat chicken, particularly chicken that had been frozen. He knelt to fetch the rock-hard chicken part and it slithered farther, until he caught it with both hands.

He handed Susannah the frozen chicken haunch, but the

gesture was ignoble, somehow. The craft launched upward, higher than Martin could imagine, like a freight lift pushed to the highest floor of a very tall building. Then, after a pause, they fell all the way down.

Susannah opened a stainless-steel door and stuck the frozen chicken part into the interior. She levered the latch, like the chrome handle in a detective show morgue. She shut the door hard.

For a long time they did not talk, their work a secret language between them. He knelt to pick up a bag of pearl rice, eye to eye with her as she wiped thawed beef juice off the galley floor with a Teflon-coated sponge. He helped, with one of those blue heavy textured rags that are famous for soaking up liquid, cubic liters of liquid, a world of fluid soaking into the cloth, even some of the rain and seawater from outside.

She put a hand out for Martin. Her fingers were clammy from picking up so many pieces of frozen food.

"We're going to have to run the ship," she said. "Probably until we get to Honolulu. Mom's not as tough as she looks."

MARTIN WAS ON DECK WHEN, with a suddenness that shocked him, the storm was nearly over.

He felt relieved and renewed. But in another part of his mind he felt dazed, the way he had not felt during the actual fury of the weather. He had been more afraid than he had let himself realize.

Sunlight broke through the clouds, and even though the seas continued to claw upward, pocked with angry foam, the wind was losing its power. Lightning flared, far off, and thunder crumpled, but the disturbance was moving on.

A greenish, beautiful light came off the ocean, day reflecting from the surface of the foam-laced water. The deck was radiant with afternoon, and the rigging sparkled with drops of water. The sea grew much calmer, and Martin thought he could see a pair of wings, a frigate bird, gliding along over the peaks of the whitecaps.

Martin took off his life jacket and suspended the garment on the hook reserved for it near the helm. There was a rule about life jackets—you had to wear them on deck at all times—but the rule was often ignored. There was a freedom about this new calm.

"The old man is resting, I take it," said Axel.

Old man. Martin had never heard this phrase from Axel before. Was Axel being affectionate and respectful, Martin wondered, or was he being quietly mocking?

"My uncle's a tough guy," said Martin.

Axel was the sort of person to sense a power vacuum on board and move in. This did not offend Martin, but he saw the possible danger of an unbridled Axel.

Claudette and Susannah came out on deck.

Claudette said, "He's asleep."

"We'll be good," said Axel, one hand on the helm, like this was at last his own personal moment.

"I know we will, Axel," said Claudette. "We'll be fine." She said this with an air of challenge, keeping Axel in his place.

"I mean that I have a lot of experience," said Axel.

"And I am sure that all your experience will prove very helpful, Axel."

To Martin her response sounded like a riposte, her words meaning just the opposite of what she said. Axel understood this. He gave a nod and a little shrug, his feelings hurt, but maybe not sure why.

She continued, "And I know you'll prove to be a model crewman—in every way."

Axel considered this. He cut his eyes over at Susannah and back at Claudette.

"Of course, Mrs. Burgess," said Axel.

Susannah stayed apart from the rest. Martin's glance kept

going back to her figure as she stood gazing out across the water, and he wondered what she was doing, what temper she had fallen into.

Susannah was listening.

But she was not listening to the conversation.

She heard a sound, but she was not able to determine what it was.

One of many difficulties inherent in being on a yacht, in Susannah's experience, was that if you lifted a hand to hang on to the stays, as the ropes supporting the masts were called, the mast swayed and the ship shifted, so you felt everything was connected to everything else.

But as she leaned out over the side of the vessel, hanging on with one hand, she had to ask herself what she was doing. Why was she clinging with one hand and leaning out over the water so that Martin and her mother both called out, concerned for her safety?

She gave no thought to herself because she did indeed hear something.

A living thing was out there on the sea.

SUSANNAH TOLD AXEL to shut off the engines.

"Please," Susannah was asking, and Axel gave an affable, reluctant nod of surrender.

Axel slowed the yacht and gradually eased it to a standstill. The engines gave a further choking clatter that finally subsided, and a whiff of exhaust peppered the wind.

The quiet was thrilling in itself, thought Martin, and as quickly as his ears took in the near silence, they also registered the many other newly apparent sounds, the sweet rush of water, lifting the powerless yacht northward, shouldering the keel, like the backs of giant, immensely powerful men. The wind whistled through the stays, and the tight-woven lines made cutting sounds, like rods of iron whipped through the air.

The fuel and water tanks made an abysmal, nearly subauditory whisper, valves opening and shutting somewhere under their feet. The *ting, ting* of something on the foremast was almost pretty—the satellite dish, dangling by a wire, apparently broken.

His own breath made a sound, and his heartbeat.

"Can you hear it?" Susannah asked.

"A seal," said Axel at last.

"Or a sea lion," said Claudette.

Martin heard it, just as everyone else did. A sound like barking, frantic barking, off the starboard bow. Martin joined Susannah leaning over the side, but the sound was hard to catch. The wind swept through the rigging, and even a gentle, wearying wind was enough to mute the sound and keep it distant.

"It's a dog," said Susannah.

"Not a dog," said Axel.

"That's what it is," said Susannah.

"Can't be," said Axel.

Martin was a little embarrassed for his cousin. The reasons why the sound of barking could not be emanating from a dog were obvious. Axel had to be right, and being right, he was not shy about making his point. He gave a lift of his chin, glad to be free of controversy.

About this, Axel's expression said, there could be no doubt.

And yet, it did sound like a dog, the sound a dog raises when he is scared, or worse. This was not the neighborly, sentry-alert sound dogs make at the approach of wandering pedestrians, but something more frightened and more insistent.

Martin said, "Yes, it sounds like a dog to me, too."

Axel nearly smiled at this, his usual have-it-your-way dismissal. "If it's a dog," he said, "the animal is in big trouble."

"It's getting closer," said Susannah.

Claudette had the binoculars to her eyes by then, searching the waves.

And then she gasped. "I can see him!"

They could all see the creature very soon, as Axel fired up the diesels and they churned forward in the direction of the struggling animal.

The seas rose up around the swimming beast, and the animal paddled frantically down the face of the ascending wave, only to vanish from sight as another wave mounted upward, blocking its path.

The approach of this failing, struggling creature galvanized the wonderstruck crew. Claudette took the helm and Axel went forward, leaned over the prow of the ship, and clapped his hands, calling out, "Come on!"

Susannah lifted a call, too, a shrill, off-key soprano, "Over here, here we are," and if there was any doubt that the dog had seen them and was making a great effort to reach them, that doubt ended when the dog vanished, lost to the surface of the sea, only to reappear again, looking drenched and forlorn. But closer, much closer, barking eagerly.

The dog was evidently a large, strong creature, able to swim upslope and plunge down the undulating seas for what must have been a very long distance. The animal fought his way, breasting the crests of the smaller waves and lunging through the spray from the whitecaps that broke around him. But there was no hint of a far-off craft that the creature might have originated from, not even an overturned hull.

And the dog was growing weak. He wasn't going to reach them, not at his current, faltering pace.

Martin knew from recent events that what happened in life was not a matter of a pleasing outcome, virtue and courage rewarded. Sometimes the deserving foundered, physically, mentally. Things went wrong.

Later Martin would wonder at his own motivation. He had no desire to drown, and no conscious desire to be extraordinarily heroic. One instant he was calling out encouragement with the rest of his fellow crew members, and the next he was shrugging a life jacket over his shoulders, fastening the garment.

Then he was over the side.

JEREMY CONTINUED TO PILOT the aircraft.

Having swung far to the east to avoid the late morning storm, the de Havilland now had to loop all the way back.

The radar screen showing the location of *Witch Grass* somewhere ahead of them was like a stew with all the solid ingredients to one side, cloud and storm far to the right, empty abyss everywhere else. Empty, except for the throbbing blister of light, the vessel's location.

Jeremy did not bother talking into the radio, trying to contact Kyle. He had given up on his friend, with a sharp sadness. Jeremy had eaten more protein bars and drunk a half liter of Fiji water. His mood had altered entirely from the assured hunter of a few hours before, and he was no longer the apprehensive pilot, either.

He had flown the plane for an hour, keeping the aircraft steady and the airspeed at right about maximum. Jeremy felt good about that.

Shako was coiled in the rear passenger seat, quiet behind his sunglasses, enduring. He was full of thoughts. He was past envying Jeremy for being able to pilot the plane, and he was weary of fantasies. Although his current favorite daydream was one in which he impressed Elwood, maybe shooting a robber trying to beat Elwood over the head at the Hilton hotel parking lot near Lihue, where the big man sometimes went to drink and pick up women.

No, Shako was determined, he would prove his worth to both of his companions in some new and inconceivable way. They would find Kyle and Paul and Laser the dog in one of those orange inflatable life rafts, swept up and down in the heavy seas. Shako would have to jump from the aircraft, like a Navy SEAL, and swim through the ocean, and as a result Mr. Tygart would not only praise Shako personally—there would be some document, several pages of legal papers, and Shako would be adopted by Mr. Tygart, and Jeremy and he would be brothers.

"I have some bad news," said Elwood.

Jeremy knew what this news was, and he did not want to hear it.

"If we don't locate them in forty-five more minutes," said Elwood, "we have to start to head back."

Back to Kauai, he meant, all the way home, hundreds of miles—defeated and without anything to show for their effort.

"No way, Elwood," said Jeremy.

Elwood put his fingers to the bill of his cap and settled the cap more firmly on his head. Jeremy added, "This is not a subject open to debate."

His dad said things like that, dealing with crooks and crooked art dealers, ex-cons and men who had murdered people. "This is not an option," he'd say, and a felon who had served twenty years for murder would back off.

Elwood looked over at him and looked away: the silent rebuke.

You didn't want to try to intimidate someone like Elwood. The truth was that Jeremy knew very little about violent death or, for that matter, plane crashes.

Although he had a pretty good feel for normal death.

His mother had drowned near Hanalei when Jeremy had been two years old. She and Ted had been drinking mai tais at the Hyatt overlooking the ocean there, leaving Jeremy with the babysitter, who eventually told him the entire story—his father never talked about it. Louise Tygart went skinny-dipping with a blood alcohol content of point one nine, took a long swim under the surf and never came back.

Jeremy had no memory of his mother, but he had more or less invented a memory. She smiled at him often, in his fictional remembrance, but she was preoccupied, wanting to go out and rake the bougainvillea or prune the hibiscus, or feed the wild mynahs, anything but endure the brisk monotony of her husband's paperwork.

Her absence had made death seem not so frightening. If the lovely, smart-looking woman in the photos around his family home could die as the result of a Saturday night frolic, then death was not only the stuff of hangmen and battlefields. Death was like those colorful coasters you put under cold drinks, or the paper you put around cupcakes, the kind you peel off, that leave a corrugated imprint.

Jeremy wondered what his mother would think of her husband's current way of life. With Ted Tygart, crime was a matter of backing up his hard drive, keeping appointments—just another business.

"It's not open to debate?" Elwood was asking amiably.

Jeremy shook his head.

"Then," Elwood said, "I guess we better find them."

Jeremy had a dreadful idea he could not shake.

He might be one of those people who are mentally challenged and don't know it. He might be one of these handicapped individuals, like those drugged-out shells who walked up and down the irrigation pipes near Hanapepe, out of their minds but not knowing it. There was no way of recognizing that you were hopeless. Hopeless people justified their lives in their own minds. He might be a fool and not know the truth about himself.

Don't come back without the money.

MARTIN REALIZED that he had made a big mistake as soon as he entered the water.

He would have been much wiser to jump, feetfirst, or to roll over the rail onto his back, as his scuba diving instructors had taught him to do. But he had plummeted headfirst, with a vigorous thrust of his legs, and this was proving awkward. Martin was helpless to direct what he did next, because he had dived into the water with such force that his downward momentum was taking a long time to lose effect.

If a frigate bird had endured the storm and had shown up to greet the afternoon sunlight, surely the loyal blue shark would not be long to make his appearance, too. If a shark, or any other hunter, wanted him, he was helpless, spinning away from the light and into the shivering darkness.

The dog would be helpless, too. The two of them would make a banquet for a starving hunter. How were you supposed to fend off a shark? Hit it on the point of its nose?

At last, several meters under the surface, he got his body turned around so that his head was uppermost. But even then, when he stopped descending, there was a long pause before the buoyancy of his life jacket began to lift him back toward the surface. And at the same time another force, his sodden denim cutoffs and the thick, surprisingly chilly water, held him down, anchored him, and made him grow even more heavy.

A stream of bubbles broke from his lips and spun upward, and then the flotation powers of the garment hoisted Martin, and he felt like a parachutist in the first, body-wrenching tug of the harness, downward progress more than halted—roughly forbidden.

He rose through the water.

The surface of the ocean still far above was a wrinkled, pulsing ceiling. Across this glaring transparency, the shape of a four-legged beast kicked, failing, its four limbs slowing down.

Martin spun upward toward the silhouette of the dog, not swimming so much as being pulled along by the life jacket, and when he broke through the ceiling of light, the air around him was alive, sea spray and the sound of wind loud in his ears.

There was no sign of the dog.

Martin sputtered, caught his breath, and called out.

"I'm over here!" he cried.

It was as though he and the dog had both kept a long-standing appointment, one that found Martin almost tardy, just barely in time. But with the waves splashing and sawing in all directions, Martin could not see the animal.

Martin waved his arms over his head, calling out again, and tried to convince himself that things were not as bad as they looked. For starters, the water was not as cold as it had felt at first. A quality of semitropical balm made the seas almost comfortable, and Martin kicked his body in the general direction of where he estimated the dog surely must be.

"Over here!" Martin called again, although there was no evident, concrete *here* in this wash of instant peaks and valleys.

And then the animal was close, a wet-spiked, wild-eyed apparition.

Martin held out his arms.

The dog rested, breathing heavily in Martin's embrace. The breath groaned in and out of the animal, and Martin could feel the creature's exhaustion. Martin could also feel his own strength striving to compensate for this new burden.

Not too heavy, Martin thought.

Not too heavy to carry to the outline of the yacht.

The vessel loomed, and the shadow of the craft fell over Martin as hands reached, and strong arms lifted both the dog and the human from the sea.

SUSANNAH SHOUTED AND WAVED encourage-
ment along with everyone else to get the big black and tan dog
out of the ocean and into the yacht. She was overwhelmed by
Martin, and gave him a hug once he was back on board, despite
the fact that he was soaked through with cold.

Axel was putting his arm around Martin next, not exactly
a hug, but a sweeping, one-armed embrace. Axel waved Claudette off, as though to say that a person this spontaneously
heroic could only be praised by a truly masculine person like
himself.

"Martin," Claudette said, "please don't risk your life like that
ever again."

Martin shivered and laughed, and agreed that he wouldn't
rescue any more dogs from the Pacific Ocean without permission.

The large dog was the wettest and most exhausted-looking
animal Susannah had ever seen, and it hurt her heart to recognize the untold story the dog represented.

Because when Susannah thought about it, the dog was an
absolute mystery. The big German shepherd was stretched out

on his side, his four legs out, and he did not look like a creature who was going to live. A puddle of water flowed out of the dog's fur, and the animal's flanks pulsed in and out with the effort of breathing.

The animal wore tags that dangled from a linked-steel choke collar, a dog license from the county of Kauai and a brass disk imprinted *Laser*.

She said the name. It was all the creature could do to open and shut his eyes, giving a thankful, companionable look toward the people gathered around him, but his tail was not wagging and his tongue lolled out like a lifeless accessory.

Susannah knelt over the animal, the dog rolling his eye toward his helper appreciatively. As Susannah examined the dog's ear, her hand came away streaked with scarlet fluid.

"Laser has been hurt," she said.

Susannah leaned to get a closer look.

"Worse than that," she added. "He's been shot."

There was a round hole just below the point of the dog's right ear, a bullet hole, maybe a nine-millimeter, a through-and-through bullet wound.

Axel brought out the backup radio scanner, a weathered Magnavox with a bent antenna. He dialed the ship-to-ship channel and asked for anyone within hearing to respond.

He got no answer. Static and hiss—but nothing else. Claudette had the binoculars up to her eyes again and swept the horizon.

Susannah felt along the dog's body, carefully, making gentle, sympathetic clucks with her mouth.

"I see the boat," said Claudette at last.

Susannah stood and gazed out across the water.

The vessel had no masts—a long, sleek-looking prow, turned away from them as the swells swept under the craft, compelling her in a northeasterly direction. The unfamiliar seacraft was a light gray hue, not that easy to distinguish from the ocean. Her entire appearance spelled trouble.

Claudette handed Susannah the binoculars.

"A powerboat," said Claudette. "What some people would call a good-sized cabin cruiser. I knew someone with a boat like that, before I knew anything about sailing."

"See anyone on board?" asked Axel.

Claudette said, "She's a ghost ship."

SUSANNAH FELT LASER'S HEARTBEAT, and she listened to the dog's weak, unsteady breathing.

The animal was aware of her and lifted his snout to give her cheek one warm lick. He laid his head down then and let out a long breath through his nostrils, and she thought: That's it. He's dead.

But he was still alive, to her great relief, and in his exhaustion he apparently still dreamed of swimming—his forepaws twitched, seeming to paddle even as he slept.

A dog's normal body temperature is one hundred degrees Fahrenheit, Susannah knew, and this dog still registered a temperature of just over ninety-five degrees. This was dangerously low, and even with all the attention she was giving it, the dog was by no means sure to survive.

Her hands were trembling with concern and outrage. Laser was suffering from hypothermia and exhaustion, and then there was the nagging loss of blood from the bullet wound. And if the dog survived the next few hours, there was the danger of pneumonia.

Axel remaining at the helm, they worked a blanket under

the dog's weight and carried the animal in this makeshift sling down into the saloon. Claudette heated beef broth—the can said *gourmet bouillon*—and Susannah set the broth beside the dog.

Martin retreated to his cabin and returned wearing a pair of khaki pants and a blue polo shirt, and he kept a towel around his shoulders, looking worried. He smiled at the dog hopefully, and looked relieved when the animal swayed to his feet, tottering on his four legs, and lapped up some of the warm broth.

Laser lay down again, heavily, and exhaled loudly. Susannah covered him with several blankets, and Claudette set out a space heater, a metal cube that radiated heat from scarlet coils.

Martin drank down the last of his own beef broth, and he asked, "Is he going to survive?"

Susannah wished that she could give Martin some good news. But at the same time he could see how she felt, how justly bitter she was. She loved Martin, and she would always admire him and be grateful to him for rescuing the dog.

But even Martin was lost in his own human nature, talkative, preoccupied, brave, and selfish. Even Martin was a human being. And for now Susannah was sick of the entire human race.

She wanted to give him a gift, reassurance that he could take in and believe, but right now there wasn't much she could offer. She wanted to be generous to Martin, and to be giving now, she had to say what she did not really feel.

"Dogs are very sturdy," Susannah said. "They are stronger

than we are, and more forgiving." Then she spoke the lie, the outright untruth, "I'm sure he'll be all right."

She could see the relief in Martin's eyes. "I sure hope so," he breathed.

Then she added something she deeply did believe.

"But someone has to be punished for this."

IN THE AFTERMATH OF THE STORM, the water had a new character, plain, wide openness that rolled outward, and then continued to gradually spread, with an apparent endlessness, toward the horizon. Martin found this hypnotic and unlike anything in his experience.

At the same time this outbound spaciousness inched upward, toward the sky. The progress of this expanse toward the zenith was slow, and the upward slope was not easy to notice. But if he glanced away for a split second and then looked back, he could perceive that the gray prairie of water had unmistakably ascended, making the sky that much less, and still less, as the climbing seascape continued to progress, until it grew entirely unmoving.

The air was all but still. But as Martin looked on, this wide moorland of water fumed, wraiths of vapor torn off by breezes that no human could sense. The spacious mesa began to shift downward, slowly, a patience-mocking process so gradual that the eye perceived it as stasis.

The unknown vessel occupied the gray-blue plain like a sharp-angled dwelling. Quiet like this, and carried by the plateau of water, the unfamiliar craft was forbidding.

Martin had more than a bad feeling.

He was fearful, and he regretted the fact that the dangling satellite dish would make a call to his parents and the rest of the world impossible.

Claudette joined Martin at the rail.

"My first boyfriend," she said, "had a boat very much like that. A Bluewater twin-diesel motor yacht. I thought Clive was the most dashing man ever born, powering around Catalina Island, using a shotgun on all the seagulls he could."

"Shooting seagulls," said Martin, "doesn't exactly sound debonair."

"When I met Leonard, I realized what a really interesting man was like, and Clive was a thing of the past. However, right now, I can say that I'm glad we have a twelve-gauge super-mag on board."

"Do you know how to use a gun?"

Claudette gave a warmhearted laugh. "My dad," she said, "taught me how to use a gun before I could ride a bike. I bagged ring-necked pheasants, quail. I was one tough little eight-year-old."

"That's reassuring," said Martin.

But Martin associated firearms with trouble—drive-by shootings and liquor store holdups.

"The problem is," Claudette was saying, "Leonard hid the shotgun in a bin somewhere, and I don't know what bin. To make matters worse, the twelve-gauge is in one locker, the shells are in another, and I have no idea where he keeps the keys."

Martin had little experience with his aunt's family, a cheerful group of men and women who wore expensive cowboy hats and handmade boots. They had owned olive orchards in the upper San Joaquin Valley and lived in turreted Victorians like gentry before the housing subdivisions tore that way of life to pieces.

"You never knew what it was like to have land," Claudette was saying. "Real land, hundreds of acres, for hunting, and riding—for anything you wanted."

Martin's parents held the mortgage on a two-story house off College Avenue in North Oakland, with one cherry tree and a lawn the size of a throw rug. He knew that Claudette meant something larger, grander than that, and he felt a twitch of resentment, her old-money attitude making Martin feel scruffy.

Claudette did not wait for him to respond. "I put my share of the inheritance into stocks with Leonard and now we have two beans to rub together."

Martin said that he was sorry to hear that.

"You," said Claudette, "don't know what sorry is."

Martin had not liked the way the mystery vessel had looked from far away.

He liked her even less up close.

MARTIN DIDN'T EVEN LIKE the vessel's name, lettered in black script across the stern, *Witch Grass, Nawiliwili, Hawaii.*

Martin thought this was not an auspicious name for a boat. She rode high in the water, her communication antennas swaying with the motion of the sea. The hull was gray rather than white, and her brass fittings had been allowed to go dull. She gave the appearance of having been abandoned for a long time—perhaps months.

Claudette used the air horn, a piercing sound that was beyond loud in Martin's ears—an unbearable noise. After several shrills from that, she used the bullhorn, starting out with a cautious "Ahoy, *Witch Grass*," sounding nautical and proper, ending up with frantic *hellos* as they drew closer.

They were close enough to hit it easily with a tennis serve when Axel cut the engine, and they drifted parallel with the silent vessel.

"I would guess she's fifty feet long, maybe fifty-five," Claudette said admiringly. "I bet she'll reach fifty or sixty knots per hour easily. She's been painted a mud color on purpose—to make her hard to see."

"Maybe someone's hurt," said Martin.

"You're right," said Claudette. "But you don't just climb on board an unfamiliar vessel. Besides, we have reason to believe that they are armed and don't mind shooting things."

"Dogs, for example," said Martin.

"For example," agreed Claudette. She switched off the bull-horn and returned it to its place in the lazarette.

"A ship's crew used to share the proceeds of a prize," prompted Axel. "In the old days."

Claudette gave Axel a smile, severe but with the hint of something new.

"We're getting ahead of ourselves," she said. "For all we know, the owners are passed out drunk and all we have to do is give them coffee and some Advil."

"But we aren't sure," said Axel.

"How much does that bother you, Axel?" asked Claudette.

Axel was aware of a challenge in Claudette's voice, something sexual and dismissive, as though Claudette might find Axel attractive, just like most other women, if she didn't have such a low regard for his character.

"It doesn't bother me at all," said Axel.

Martin knew that he was lying. The strange vessel disturbed all of them.

As they drew even closer, they could see further signs of trouble.

A constellation of bullet holes punctured the side windows of the cabin. What looked like red paint was splashed down from the helm, along the hull. And an outline showed along the boat's rail, like a red glove that had been folded over the side. But this was not a glove.

It was a bloody handprint.

THIS EVIDENCE OF VIOLENCE hushed them.

As the yacht edged closer to the powerboat, Martin felt cold—he wanted to be miles away. And yet, his conscience reminded him, what if someone has been shot and is too feeble to call out?

When they got closer, the streamlined bulk of the power cruiser bucked, a surge of wind catching the two vessels. *Athena's Secret* moved close, and the two crafts collided.

The crash was powerful enough to make Martin stagger, and Axel was quick to reverse the engines, backing the sailing vessel out of the way. The masts and the rigging swayed, and the yacht shrugged and shuddered along her length.

"I'm not afraid to board her unarmed," said Axel. "How about you, Martin?"

"Wait," said Claudette, "until we find where Leonard keeps the shotgun."

"Looking for the gun might take a long time," said Axel. "A boat like this carries valuables."

He seemed to like that word, because he said it again.

"Valuables that could be ours. If Martin wants to listen to his aunt's advice, I'll go right ahead all by myself."

Martin's pride required him to say, "I'll go, too."

Belowdecks, Laser was drowsily awake, lifting his head to see who was passing by. Susannah had made her patient a bed in a corner of the cabin, with a buffer of rolled-up quilts. Laser was a handsome animal, with tawny forepaws and flecks of gold in his coffee-colored eyes.

"Sorry about the little boating accident," said Martin, adding a brief explanation of what was happening.

The dog licked the air in the direction of Martin's voice and settled his head back down.

"Martin," Susannah said, "don't take any more risks than you have to."

Martin took three yellow and black Motorola walkie-talkies out of the equipment case, along with a couple of flashlights. "It's a deal," he said.

Martin was weak-kneed from the collision, and the effort of rescuing the dog had left him feeling drained. He was not ready to investigate anything, much less an unknown craft in the middle of the ocean. But he did not imagine Leonard recovering anytime soon.

"Axel will talk you into trouble, Martin," she said.

Martin clipped a two-way radio to his belt.

He said, "It's not that simple."

* * *

Claudette took the helm and eased the yacht closer.

Steering the yacht was more halting now, because Claudette was using exaggerated care, afraid of another crash. She gunned the engines, nearly stalling them, swinging the stern too close, backing up too quickly.

Claudette kept the yacht in place only long enough for Martin to clamber up and over the rail of the other craft. Axel joined him, making a point of not needing a helping hand, the two of them half climbing, half stumbling onto *Witch Grass*.

MARTIN KEPT HIS BACK TO THE SEA, leaning against the side of the vessel.

He had never been less happy to be anywhere. Maybe Susannah was right. Maybe it was that simple: Axel had talked him into trouble.

Axel waited right beside him. Martin turned to gaze at *Athena's Secret*. He could see his fellow crew members, people who had become so familiar. How alive with curiosity they both looked, thought Martin. Claudette gave a wave. Martin drank in the sight of the beautiful yacht, her two masts red in the afternoon sunlight.

"Blood," said Axel.

Martin followed his gaze.

Axel added, "And more blood."

Red matter was spattered all the way up the steps to the helm, as far as Martin could tell without moving from where they stood. A splotchy, air-darkened trail of blood led into the cabin, where a door was held open, fastened by a bungee cord. The empty doorway was dark, with a wedge of sunlight that shifted as the vessel moved.

Martin called out, a cheerfully singsong *hello*. They listened for a response that did not come.

The cruiser had a different layout than the yacht, with two chairs in the stern, bolted into place, presumably for fishing. The helm, what Martin could see of it, was forward and up on the cabin, protected by a Plexiglas windscreen and a sunroof. The interior of the cabin, and whatever lay belowdecks, remained to be seen.

The vessel had an unfamiliar motion, too, swaying from side to side and pitching unpredictably, even in the relatively calm water. The deck was teak, weathered but high quality, seventeen or eighteen feet across, with a stainless-steel cargo hatch. The hatch had a small Plexiglas skylight, and the two of them knelt, peering into the dark interior, using their flashlights.

They could see nothing except for the answering circles of their two flashlights, several feet below. The smell in the air was of something that had burned—seared electronics and ozone.

"Empty," said Axel. "No wonder she floats so high in the water.

A storage compartment, a metal trunk, was set into the vessel's aft, and Martin opened it. He saw what appeared to be a bright orange Avon life raft, folded and compressed, exactly as it had left the factory.

Their walkie-talkies sputtered and chattered, Claudette's voice sounding comically diminished.

"It smells like they had a lightning strike," Martin told his aunt. "The storm probably knocked out their ignition, maybe killed their engine."

"Do you see any survivors?" Claudette asked, sounding like someone far away, on the other side of the planet.

"Not exactly," said Martin.

"Martin, tell me what you see."

"The life raft is still on board, unopened," said Martin, "so it doesn't look like they safely abandoned ship."

He didn't want to mention all the blood. He felt squeamish, but that was not the problem. Talking about the blood made it more real, and more unavoidable, and brought Martin closer to actually setting eyes on evidence of death.

But Claudette was persistent. "Do you see any more signs of trouble?"

"We're taking care of it," said Martin.

"How are we going to do this?" Axel asked when Martin had reassured his aunt that they would report every significant observation and replaced the walkie-talkie onto his belt.

"You're a lot more courageous than I am," said Martin. His voice was a raspy noise he scarcely recognized as his own. "I'll go check out the helm," said Martin. "And you—"

"You want me to look at the cabin?" said Axel.

Axel was deferring to Martin, letting him take the lead, and Martin appreciated this. He also realized that this kept Axel in Martin's favor. It also guaranteed that if anything went wrong, it could be blamed on Martin.

"Be careful," said Martin.

MARTIN CLIMBED THE STEPS to the pilot house, forward on the cabin structure.

The steps were slathered in darkening blood—more of the stuff than Martin would have thought possible. He crept up the side of the steps, clinging to the rail to avoid stepping in the gore.

The pilot house was high, overlooking the prow and the ocean, and swayed even more drastically from side to side than the rest of the vessel.

He smelled the dead body before he saw it.

The man was not dead so much as completely reduced from a living being to a lifeless assembly of limbs and clothing. He wore a puka shell necklace, a blue all-weather poncho, and a pair of Levi's, with black K-Swiss running shoes. His jaws were parted, exposing a steel tooth.

Martin examined the details of the clothing carefully because he did not want to look directly at what else was there—the man's face and the rain-diluted blood on the metal grid of the flooring.

The pilot house was designed to give the impression that

the vessel was a spaceship. A tall seat upholstered in black leather overlooked a console with a computer screen and many dials, along with a Lowrance sonar fish finder. A radio was built into a console, the entire setup more sport- and fishing-oriented than anything on *Athena's Secret*. A side chest of melting ice was packed with Red Bull and Dos Equis. Many of the cans were empty.

A Panasonic transponder was attached to the underside of the console, a metal box with a glowing red light, no doubt kept working by battery power. Otherwise, none of the equipment was turned on, or else the electricity was out, flash-burned by lightning.

Martin called to Axel, but his voice was too weak with the strain of his discovery. He called again, and at last used his most piercing whistle, two fingers in his mouth.

When Axel appeared from inside the cabin his lips were set in a grim line, an upside-down smile, and his cheeks had new shadows.

"Come up here," was all Martin could say.

Axel carried himself carefully, putting his hand on the rail as he came up the stairs in uncharacteristic caution.

Martin stood aside so Axel could take a look.

Axel was silent. He plainly did not like what he was looking at, either, but he knelt beside the dead guy's handgun, a large automatic lying on the crosshatched, slip-proof-metal flooring of the pilot house.

"A Glock nine-millimeter," said Axel. "This is the guy who tried to shoot the dog."

"He did," said Martin.

"Did what?" asked Axel, rising to his feet. He had the pistol in his hand, across the flat of his palm.

Martin's voice was trembling, and he clung to literal truthfulness, forcing his mind to endure one detail at a time. "He did shoot the dog, apparently."

Axel briefly removed the ammunition clip, examined it, and slid it back in. "Two bullets left," he said, tucking the Glock into the top of his denims.

"What about fingerprints, Axel?" said Martin.

"You mean," said Axel, his voice flat, "when the homicide detectives and the crime scene unit show up, I might be in trouble."

Martin did not respond to this.

Axel said, "There's a dead guy in the cabin, too."

THE CABIN WAS POORLY LIT, once they got beyond the angle of daylight thrown by the open door. The space smelled wrong—unhealthy and overripe, but not as bad, Martin surmised, as it would in a few more hours.

There was enough illumination to allow Martin to briefly examine the other body. It was clad in a hooded Nike jogging jacket, khaki cargo pants, and Converse basketball shoes. The body was on its side, wedged between a cabinet and a fixed-in-place barstool. The dead guy's left hand held an iPhone, and a handgun lay in a corner nearby, a revolver.

Martin did not mind looking as this corpse so much, because the light was muted and he was perhaps already getting used to this sort of thing. Or so he told himself. He touched the body. It was clammy, and it was stiff, too, the arm rigid where Martin nudged it. And there was that growing dead smell here in the enclosed space that he had not noticed so strongly in the partially open structure of the pilot house.

Martin was very sorry he had disturbed the corpse's repose, and he nearly apologized out loud. He felt particularly troubled because this person had been trying to contact help, probably, using the handheld device. How terrible it was, thought Martin, to die so dismally, out in the ocean. He said a prayer—a spontaneous, unspoken *God help these people.*

Martin picked up the revolver.

He held the firearm very cautiously, and carried it into the doorway. He did what he had seen detectives do in movies, swinging the cylinder out, and letting the shells spill into his hand. The copper shells were all empty—the unknown man had fired every bullet in the gun.

Axel wasn't talking, and Martin kept his mouth shut, too. He put the revolver down next to the DVD player. His flashlight beam joined Axel's in probing the interior. The lights shifted from shelf to floor to galley. The place was sparsely furnished, but what was there was quality—a Sony LCD hi-def screen, a Bosch freezer and ice maker, with what looked like teak paneling on the walls.

The walkie-talkie on Martin's hip was making a tiny squawking sound, like a transmission from deep space—Claudette's questioning voice. Martin turned down the volume. He didn't want to talk about any of this, ever, if he could help it.

Martin examined the living quarters. There was a liquor cabinet, the bottles held in place by a crossbar, gin and tequila. An Apple laptop lay closed on a side shelf, and the DVDs were all X-rated and action movies. He found two metal dishes on a bottom shelf, beside a neatly folded bag of Natural Balance Ultra Premium dog kibble.

For a fairly expensive pleasure craft, there was a lot of

unused space and few partitions. The living area opened aft into a cargo hold. Where Martin would have expected sleeping quarters or even enclosed cabins, there was emptiness, with heavy-duty bungee cords attached to the walls, the kind shippers use to hold cargo in place.

In the daylight that fell down through the skylight in the hatch, it was evident that the vessel had once carried a shipment, but now she was empty.

Axel found a small door panel near the freezer and he asked Martin to hold a light on the thing while he switched circuit breakers off and on. He asked Martin to experiment with the wall switches, too, but the chamber remained dark.

"Generator," said Axel. "Must be fried."

"Can we get her running again?"

"Sure," said Axel. "Have to jump-start the engines."

"So this boat isn't permanently—" Martin could not bring himself to say *dead in the water.*

Martin had the absurd feeling that the dead person would hear the phrase and be offended.

"Not permanently," said Axel.

He opened the fridge and sorted through the dark interior. "Beef patties," he said. "Lasagna. Still pretty much frozen."

He unscrewed the cap of a bottle of tequila and sniffed it, as though suspicious. He did not drink any of it.

"What do you think happened?" asked Martin.

"They shot each other," said Axel.

"How?" Martin had learned how to think like this, working

with scientists at Scripps—theorize about what hunting fish had taken a bite out of the sea bass, measure the bite, estimate how long ago the bass had escaped.

"We can guess," said Axel. He found a toolbox on a shelf and sorted through wrenches and wiring.

"I think the bald puka shell guy shot the iPhone guy first," said Martin. "The dog got upset, tried to protect his master, and then he got shot, too."

Axel found a socket wrench and spun it around, the ratcheting noise loud in the enclosed space.

"The iPhone guy wasn't dead," Martin continued. "He staggered up to the helm, and the puka shell guy blew most of the rest of his clip trying to defend himself, getting killed anyway. Then iPhone guy crawled back down here and died. That explains the two paths of blood on the stairs and the bullet holes in the Plexiglas—puka shell guy did not have a very good aim."

Axel nodded. "Sounds about right," he said.

"It all happened this morning, early," said Martin. "Rigor mortis is just beginning to wear off." Dead fish got rigor, and so did most other creatures, Martin had learned. Thinking analytically like this, Martin discovered, made the crimes just a little less upsetting.

"Good theory," said Axel.

"But," continued Martin, "what were they fighting over?"

"People fight," said Axel.

Martin gently kicked a sports bag on a lower shelf, the kind of carryall people use for tennis equipment and gym clothes.

He leaned down and poked it with his fingers, then he hooked the bag—which was surprisingly heavy—and set it down in the wedge of daylight.

The outside of the bag was flame-red, and it featured a logo, Sleeping Giant Gym and Spa, with yellow lettering. Martin tugged the zipper.

Martin's understanding of the recent violence became instantly more clear. He could see, now, the possible grounds for the two homicides.

The bag was full of money.

THE MONEY WAS in the form of bundles of hundred-dollar bills, each held together with a light blue paper band. Each paper band, as far as Martin could tell at a glance, had been carefully defaced with a black marker to disguise the bank name and other identification.

No sooner had Martin set his eyes on this money than he had the impulse to hide it from Axel.

Martin had no particular reason to expect Axel to seize the money, or in any way behave dishonorably, but a hoard of this size changed the way Martin felt about his companion, and about his own personal future.

This wasn't the promise of money, like a future paycheck or an inheritance. This was actual money, right here, giving off the admirable but unfamiliar whiff of old printed paper, hand-worn, conserved, and refolded many times. *Mine.* The word was like a neon pulse in his head.

But it was too late to hide.

Axel was already kneeling beside the bag and running his hands down into it. He pulled out a bundle of cash and stood in the doorway. He fanned the currency like a deck of cards and held one of the bills to the daylight through the doorway without removing it from the stack, like a prospective book buyer admiring a printed page.

Martin waited for what Axel was about to say, but he could guess the words.

So when they came, Martin was not very surprised.

"We could split this," said Axel. "Just you and me."

He knelt again, joining Martin on his knees beside the money. To make his meaning clear, he added, "I mean that we could keep this. All of it."

The two of them remained on their knees beside their discovery.

"We could," agreed Martin.

But he felt again how unwise it was to discuss such things with Axel. Retreating from his feeling of personal greed, Martin was convinced that what he really wanted was to give the money to his uncle, and let the cash end up being shared with the entire crew.

"We could keep it," said Martin, "but we won't."

Axel put the bundle of money back into the bag and hefted the bag in both hands, like a traveler trying to remember if he had packed his underwear. "This must weigh forty pounds."

"At least," Martin agreed.

"You're not thinking, Martin," said Axel. "We could set this money to one side. Hide it."

"How?"

"Or, we could report to Mr. and Mrs. Burgess that we found

the money after we had already kept some of it back. As a commission, like."

"A finder's fee," suggested Martin.

Axel smiled. But this was a new, unfamiliar smile, a just-you-and-me, confidential grin. Axel was aglow, enjoying this. "Right. A finder's fee."

It made sense in a way. Martin felt how exciting it was, the two of them in on a grand secret. "How much do you think it is?"

Axel shook his head. "A lot."

"How much?"

Axel thought about this, running mental calculations. "If they are all hundred-dollar bills," he said, "this is a fortune."

The words went through Martin like an electric current.

"Of course," said Martin, "this might all be counterfeit."

"The C-note I looked at had a watermark."

"You're an expert at identifying money?" asked Martin.

"I play cards with strangers," said Axel. "Someone pays you money, you give it a good look. This is the real thing." Axel put his hand out to touch Martin's chest, and leaned forward. "I have debts, Martin," he continued. "Money like this would mean a lot."

Martin was caught at that instant by a compelling possibility. He could have all this money himself. Why did he even have to share this cash with Axel? A shocking accident could happen, and Axel could hit his head.

This instant fantasy, Martin with the entire satchel of

money, was a waking reverie that could have lasted a long time. Axel would be gone, and Martin and the rest could have a nice long talk about things being different.

Axel was the one who shook Martin to his senses when he said, in an offhand way, "Of course, I'm the one with a loaded gun. Why do I have to share this with you?"

Martin said, "You're talking about shooting me."

AXEL WAS NOT SMILING NOW.

He was back to his usual expression of masculine endurance.

"Maybe," he admitted. "Maybe I am raising the possibility."

"The possibility of using the gun to kill me," persisted Martin.

Axel kept his voice even, and his answer short. "Just talking."

Martin was quiet, but he was appalled. "You're looking me right in the face and threatening my life."

Martin knew that if he was going to hurt Axel, disable or stun him in order to defend himself, it would have to be now.

Axel lifted both hands in denial.

Martin shook his head in disbelief. But it was not total disbelief. Martin himself had briefly entertained the same impulse. "You're saying that you would murder me to keep this."

Axel looked away and lifted one shoulder.

Then he looked back at Martin. There was a trace—a bare hint—of a smile in his eyes when he said, "I scared you, didn't I?"

"Yes, and you still do," said Martin.

"There are people I would kill to keep this money, Martin," Axel said, "but you aren't one of them."

"How can I believe you?"

"It's the money doing this to us," said Axel. "We find some money in a gym bag and we turn into a couple of criminals."

"I don't know if I can turn my back on you," said Martin.

"Now you're starting to offend me, Martin," said Axel. "A guy like you doesn't get killed by Axel Owen over a sack of money."

Martin felt his body begin to relax.

"Also," added Axel, "I need you. Aside from me, you're the only one strong enough to work the yacht's rigging winch if the power goes out."

Martin zipped the carrier tightly.

Then he and Axel went out under the open sky, and Martin turned up the volume of his walkie-talkie.

Across the water Claudette was intoning directions into the two-way radio. "I am really upset, Martin. Very, very upset. You told me you would keep in constant communication."

Martin said that he was sorry and added that he had some news. He had heard the formula before and never liked it. But he used the phrase when he added, "I have some good news, and some bad news."

Claudette was quick to ask, "Is anyone hurt?"

"I'm OK and Axel is OK," said Martin. "But there are two dead people on the boat."

This news shut her up for one long moment.

"Dead how?" asked Claudette.

"Shot, as far as we can tell," said Martin. "That's the bad news. The good news is, we found some money."

Claudette's voice sounded doubtful. She was in no hurry, absorbing this fresh information. "What do you mean, *money*?"

Martin was at that moment aware of a sound from the sky.

An aircraft was approaching.

THE NOISE WAS A LOW-KEY, pleasing growl, the sort of far-off engine sound Martin associated with small airports and Sunday afternoons, amateur pilots enjoying unlimited visibility. He was happy to see this sign of civilization, someone enjoying the Pacific from the air. He envied the pilot, and wished that he, too, was looking down from a great height.

The airplane was still very far away.

Martin shaded his eyes, watching the red and white aircraft catch the afternoon illumination.

"The same plane Susannah and Claudette saw," Axel said thoughtfully. "You know what that means?"

Martin asked what it meant.

"It isn't flying from point A to point B," said Axel. "It's looking for something—searching."

"Looking for a shipwreck?" asked Martin.

"No, not just a wreck," said Axel. "The emergency radio channels have been quiet."

Axel let this thought sink in. Then he said, "Let's hurry up and get the money off this boat."

Martin sensed the beginnings of alarm in Axel's voice, but they both relaxed when the aircraft headed along a path that took it well away from the two vessels. Its flight continued westward, and it diminished to a distant, gnatlike speck, so far away that the sound became inaudible.

The airplane was gone, or so nearly vanished that it did not matter. Martin would have liked to see the aircraft dip its wings in response to a cheerful wave from the crew members. That would have been reassuring.

And at the same time, the plane's departure visibly allayed Axel's anxiety, allowing him to shrug and shake his head cheerfully. The pilot of the red and white aircraft either had not seen them or he was deeply indifferent to the lives of sailing folk and their vessels.

Over on the yacht, Claudette had the binoculars to her eyes, watching the vanishing point where the aircraft turned to empty sky.

She lowered the binoculars and said something to Susannah, handing her the field glasses and running her hands up and down her arms, adjusting the roll of her sleeves, something she did when she was nervous or preoccupied. Martin could not read her exact words, but when she pointed to the sky and waved her arm back and forth, it was obvious she was worried about the aircraft.

Athena's Secret approached, Claudette at the helm, and the engines churned the water as the two hulls grew close, and even closer, until there was the slightest nudge.

Axel leaped onto the yacht first, turning to take the money securely from Martin's hands.

Martin had the most arresting impulse—he should let the

heavy weight fall into the shifting water between the two vessels. The act of fumbling the carrier away would be easy, and it would resolve all the potential turmoil.

Axel's hands made the encouraging, silently excited urging Martin associated with basketball games, *come on*.

Martin could easily imagine what his portion of the money would buy. He could give his dad a new tennis racket, one of the new models made of carbon and space plastic. He could buy his mother a new Epson printer, and he could buy a new microscope for himself, a Bausch and Lomb binocular model he could use to study diatoms and plankton. His entire family would be happier because of this money.

So before he could fling the money away, his hands were operating on autopilot, handing the heavy bag over to Axel, who gathered it in and held it like a man holding a living creature, fragile and easily hurt.

Axel kept the bag in an embrace, stepping carefully over to Claudette and making the exchange with her, as though not wanting to give the money to anyone else just yet.

Claudette herself made a exclamation of surprise. The bag was too heavy to be held easily.

She set the bag down and looked into it, like a woman reluctantly and cautiously peering down into a container that might explode.

Martin waited while Axel got a line and cast it across.

Martin used a bowline knot around a cleat to join *Witch Grass* to *Athena's Secret*.

But as he did this, he was aware that to an observer, this act of tying the two seacraft together meant that the two would travel as one. It also meant that Martin and his crewmates were taking possession of this abandoned craft. The act was clear, and it was significant.

Martin felt a stirring of unease as the yacht backed away to avoid a lunge on the part of the lurching, unstable power cruiser.

He wanted to get off *Witch Grass* as soon as he could. He felt the sinister, unclean presence of the dead men. He wanted to have a mug of hot cocoa and let Claudette and Leonard, when he felt better, make the decisions. But he was aware that they were about to undertake an act of possession that was not entirely right. Towing the vessel was not the problem, although the yacht would have a slow trip, pulling *Witch Grass* until Axel could get the engine started.

The problem was that they were taking a large amount of money that did not belong to them.

No matter how he turned their actions around in his mind, and no matter how he tried to pretend to himself, he could not hide one basic fatal defect in what they were doing.

They were stealing.

JEREMY FELL ASLEEP.

He was not aware of drowsing.

But he was aware of a physiological slide that led him little by little to the point of muddled oblivion. He simply stopped being able to hold his eyes open as the translucent, vibrant disk of the propeller blades continued rotating on and on, and the sea crawled—inched, stood still—beneath them.

They had maybe ten minutes to go before fuel shortage forced them to turn back and begin the long retreat to Kauai. Jeremy believed that if he ever did have the opportunity to set his two feet on the planet again, he would walk into the ocean with his clothes on. He would not strip down to his bathing trunks, or get naked, he would just walk right out into the water out of sheer extravagance.

Look, he would say to the ocean, I am so glad to be back on earth that I don't care. He would walk out under the breaking surf, holding his breath. He would stand in the breakers at Poipu Beach, and he would be happy.

And so his eyelids grew very heavy. They were eyelids of

lead, coverings of the most oppressively weighty material ever crafted. No one could keep such eyelids open.

And he lost all contact with where he was, and he slept.

Then something or someone was jostling Jeremy's arm, and he stirred. Elwood was pointing to the side, his forefinger up and down like a bird's beak, insistently.

"There they are," said Elwood.

Jeremy fumbled for the binoculars.

"There's that pretty ketch alongside her," said Elwood.

Jeremy must have looked puzzled.

"That cute two-masted yacht," continued Elwood. "She's pulled alongside *Witch Grass*, and I bet they are helping themselves to the money."

The two vessels were tiny from this altitude, the powerboat looking chunky and capable, the yacht looking sleek and delicate. The two were more than right beside each other—they seemed joined, two dissimilar halves of a single floating craft. Through the binoculars Jeremy could see people, a tall woman, and a shorter one.

And there was someone on *Witch Grass*, some guy with reddish brown hair and a dark T-shirt, not Kyle and not Paul. A trespasser. Jeremy stirred in his seat, unable to restrain his impatience.

"We have to stop them," he said.

"Yes, we do," Elwood agreed.

But Elwood was in no hurry. He gave the aircraft some throttle and flew directly west, away from their discoveries.

"What we need to do," Elwood said, "is consider how lucky we are."

"How lucky are we?" asked Jeremy, mystified.

"That's one of those yachts collectors are crazy about, designed by Bill what's-his-name, Ingbord. A ship like that is worth millions of dollars even on the black market. The kind of people your dad does business with would kill to own one of those."

"OK," said Jeremy, not sure what a collector would do with a stolen yacht. Maybe keep it in dry dock and hold parties on it.

"Pleasure boats often don't carry guns, in my experience," said Elwood. "Even when they have a shotgun or a .45 secured with a gun lock, they are slow to use them. Rich folks hire people like me to protect them."

"That's good," said Jeremy, baffled. Personally, he would never hire Elwood to do anything. He was too intimidating and given to conversations like this, telling someone younger and more ignorant what to do.

Elwood said, "You'll come out of this a new man, Jeremy."

"OK," said Jeremy unsteadily, thinking that *a new man* was not exactly what he wanted to be.

"But," said Elwood, "I am going to need your help. You and Shako, both."

Jeremy felt a small flicker of disquiet. "We're just going to get the money, right?"

"And the yacht," said Elwood.

"How?" asked Jeremy, feeling that he was really not smart enough to be a hands-on criminal. That was the trouble with his dad's business. Electronic transfers were always being made to banks in Panama, and Dad was always meeting with his tax lawyer. You had to be smart.

"Look in that carryall down at your feet," said Elwood. "Take out that zip-bag."

Jeremy reached in among the flares and duct tape and pulled out the heavy black zipped bag. He'd been uneasily curious about this all day.

"Unzip it," said Elwood.

The scent of the interior of the ballistic nylon case was gun oil, an earthy, reassuring smell, unless you knew anything about guns. The weapon was a pug-nosed piece of equipment, all trigger and stock. Jeremy had seen pictures online: the Ingram MAC-10.

"Fires thirty-two rounds a second," said Elwood. "You tuck it under your shirt, bring it out, and rip."

Rip would be about right. The gun scared Jeremy.

"Mr. Quinn," called Elwood, "I want you to get ready now. We have the Ingram prepared, and you need to wake up."

Shako reached out between the seats, holding his hand out, flexing his fingers. *Give me the gun.*

"When we have completed our descent, Mr. Quinn, you'll get the weapon," said Elwood.

Jeremy looked back at Shako, and the killer had his sunglasses off, cleaning them with one of those little squares of cloth you get at the optometrist. His green eyes looked at Jeremy, and his lips gave that tight little straight-line smile.

Elwood powered the aircraft to a greater speed and then banked the plane, the blue water slab tilting to one side while the cockpit and its occupants seemed to stay level.

Jeremy felt that his words were powerless, drowned out by the grinding sound of the engine as he insisted, "But we aren't going to hurt any more people than we have to."

Elwood gave Jeremy a long chance to look at his stony profile, saying nothing.

Then, as the aircraft leveled off again, he said, "Jeremy, just what kind of business do you think your dad is in?"

LASER WAS STILL ALIVE.

Susannah knew that the animal was grateful for her attention because he followed her with his eyes whenever she got up to refresh the contents of the hot water bottle, or to get another quilt from her cabin and throw it over the dog's recumbent form.

Susannah put her hand on Laser's flank, adjusted the blanket over his still-damp body, and said, "What were you struggling to get away from?"

There was an answer, but it was an unknowable answer, hidden in the instinctive Tao of the dog's nature. When Susannah got up to find the hair dryer in her cabin, the dog looked up apprehensively, and when she returned she reassured the animal.

"I'll be here," she said. "All afternoon and all night, as long as you need me, I'll be right here."

The hair dryer was a Bespoke Labs professional model, one that Leonard had joked would blow the circuits on the yacht. She used it to dry and then fluff the dog's hair, and he lifted his head and licked at the warm blast of air that came out of the strange device.

Then she sat with the dog, listening to the rise and fall of his breathing.

Fatigue, the dog would have said. *Very great fatigue is all I am feeling right now. And gratitude.*

"What did they find on the boat?" Susannah asked.

"Dead bodies," said Claudette.

Susannah nearly said, *I'm glad to hear it.* She wanted the people who had hurt this animal to suffer.

Laser lifted his head and pricked up his healthy ear, the wounded ear remaining partly folded over. She had bandaged it, and the bandage had weight.

He whined. This was not a whine of curiosity, or lonesomeness, or any other minor emotion Susannah could recognize in a dog's whimper.

The dog heard something that aroused his fear.

Continuingly alert to this sound, the dog was no longer the incapable, badly stricken patient. He growled. Wobbly but fierce, the animal climbed to his feet, and his hackles rose, a ridge of fur down his spine. He bared his teeth, and even in his weakened condition the dog looked ferocious.

Susannah was very puzzled and deeply disturbed. She went to the cabin door and opened it.

Far off, almost too faint for human ears, she could barely make out the drone of an airplane as the dog snarled a warning.

"LEONARD, WAKE UP," Susannah said as Claudette gave her husband a gentle shake.

"I am awake," he replied, but he held himself on top of the blankets like a man caught by a photograph in midair, his knees crooked, his arms at an angle, unmoving. He did not look relaxed.

And he did not open his eyes. Everything about the man communicated pain, and also indicated the faith that if he did not move, not so much as a single eyelid, he would be able to control the worst of his suffering.

Susannah realized how much her father meant to her. And she also realized that getting rid of the boat, and maybe doing without a wife and a daughter, might simplify his life and bring his energetic, exacerbated soul a new experience.

Her parents had been sleeping in separate bunks, Leonard the lower shelf, and Susannah could see the differences between the two of them. Leonard was all sprawl, lying next to a classical Greek dictionary flowering with blue Post-its, and *Jane's Fighting Ships*, stuck with bookmarks.

Her mother was tidy—even the Kleenex had a covering,

a magenta plastic box with a timid leaf of facial tissue barely protruding. Her mother liked true crime, books about dingoes that ate children, and serial killers.

The victims were always women, the killers always men. A paperback called *Serpentine* had escaped and lay in a corner, and her mother knelt now and picked it up and put it back where it belonged.

Claudette bent down over her husband. "Leonard," she said, "we found some money."

Susannah wanted to correct her mother. Martin found the money, and Axel found it with him. But she saw the need in her mother's eye, the glow and the anxiety that that newfound wealth gave her. Claudette was thrilled but she was uneasy. Now she had something else in addition to an injured husband and an expensive yacht that she could lose.

Her mother's life could be simplified, too. Claudette was always on the verge of happiness—rarely purely, brilliantly happy. Even now, waiting for Leonard to respond, she could not wait, and she leaned down over her husband and said, "A lot of money."

Leonard parted his lips. He was preparing his body for pain, and for conversation. Sometimes, thought Susannah, almost the same thing. Especially, she thought, around me.

He opened one eye.

"Money?" he croaked.

"That's what I said," Claudette responded, impatient but in control of her emotions.

He opened the other eye. He blinked. "How much?"

"We don't know yet. It's a lot."

He gave a surprised laugh, his mouth wide open.

"But it is not quite that simple," said Claudette.

"What is simple?" he asked. "In the whole world, name me one thing that is absolutely straightforward."

Claudette described the forsaken vessel, giving Leonard the facts, and Susannah respected the shorthand verve with which she spoke: dead bodies, an apparent falling-out between thieves.

"And now," she concluded, like she was sharing entirely good news, "we have the cash."

"Dead!" said Leonard. In Susannah's experience, he always responded emotionally to bad news, disaster or death on TV. "That's terrible!"

"We have the cash, Leonard," Claudette repeated, to emphasize her main point. "American money, legal tender."

"OK," he said. "Salvage rights are ours."

"Are you sure?" said Claudette.

"The vessel was abandoned, right?" he asked.

"In effect," said Claudette.

"What does that mean, *in effect?*" he responded. "We found the money on a vessel abandoned on the high seas. The vessel and everything on it are claimable."

"But not beyond dispute," said Claudette.

"Is there a problem?"

Now she mentioned the aircraft.

"Oh." Leonard considered this. His *oh* was weighted with feeling. He needed to think.

He looked at Susannah, and he looked back at his wife.

Susannah could imagine his thoughts, the need to protect wife and daughter from the kind of felons Claudette liked to read about.

"Well, yes," he said at last, sounding thoughtful, "I can see the difficulty."

"I've watched it off and on all day," said Claudette. "The plane is searching."

"Searching for what, though?" he asked.

Claudette asked, "Where is the key to the overhead cabinet?"

He offered a feeble laugh. "Trapped in my hip pocket."

Claudette said, "We need the shotgun."

"What you need," said Leonard, "is me."

Claudette folded her arms, needing her husband, and liking him, too, but nonetheless there was the unresolved problem between them.

Susannah wondered if her mother wanted with all her heart to get her hands on all the money, every last piece of currency, and talk divorce from a position of strength.

"NO, WE DON'T NEED YOU," said Claudette. "We need the shotgun and the ammunition."

"Do you realize," said Leonard, "how worse than useless the shotgun is?"

"Useless how?" asked Claudette, shifting the weight off her weak leg.

"If these people are showing up to claim their money," said Leonard, "and they ask for it, and know we have it—we should give it back."

"We aren't giving back this money, Leonard."

"And if these are armed men, ready to take what they want, then we should give it back to protect ourselves."

"We'll keep the money," said Claudette.

"If these are professional criminals with the ability to hunt the money with an airplane," continued Leonard, "we'd be better off ditching the cash, throwing it overboard. We don't want to kill people, Claudette."

"You always said you wanted to find a fortune," Susannah told him, "floating on the waves."

"I was hoping for hatch covers, cordage. Maybe a mast, or planking, some nice spruce wood. But this money is dangerous."

"Maybe Mother would feel better," suggested Susannah, "if she had the gun in her hands." She used the word *mother* deliberately, acting as a levelheaded but cunning referee between her parents.

"That's right, Leonard," said Claudette.

"Oh, Claudette." Leonard was surrendering—Susannah could hear it in his voice. But she could also hear stark apprehension. "This is such a bad idea."

"The keys, Leonard," Claudette persisted.

He altered his position, gasping.

Susannah found the keys in his back pocket, two yellow keys on a California Golden Bears key ring, warm from contact with her father's body.

Father and daughter could hear the overhead compartments in the center cabin opening and closing, and the sound of the gun being taken down was audible, too, the thud of the stock on the floor.

Claudette carried the gun, zippered up in a gun case, back into the sleeping quarters. She also carried four green and gold boxes, and she set the gun and ammunition on the floor. She unzipped the shotgun and tore open a box.

"I thought you bought buckshot," she said.

"Why do you think I keep the guns locked up?" asked Leonard. "Those slugs could bring down a grizzly."

"Five rounds per box. I've got twenty slugs."

Susannah noted the *I've got*. But taking possession of the gun with its glowing walnut stock made Claudette somber. She sank to the floor, loading the gun, taking her time.

"It's not that much fun," said Leonard, "when you actually lay hands on the gun, is it?"

"All of this scares me, too," said Claudette. "I have to ask if I really want to shoot someone."

"Yeah, well, that's a very good question, Claudette," said Leonard. "I'm glad to hear that you still have enough sense to speculate."

Claudette gave him a smile, knowing and gently teasing. "I thought you liked that about me, Leonard," she said. "That I'm full of surprises."

"I do," said Leonard.

Something passed between the two of them. They were not easy on each other, Susannah could see, but the prospect of having an adventure, getting involved in a conspiracy on the high seas, was beginning to tantalize Leonard.

"When you set eyes on the money, Leonard," said Claudette, "you'll want to keep it, too."

"YOU DIDN'T HAVE an affair with Michelle, did you, Leonard?" Susannah asked when Claudette had left them alone.

She knew how it must shock her father to hear the question put so bluntly. But Susannah did not mind shocking anyone, not even Leonard.

He ignored her question. "Susannah, I need you to give me a shot of morphine," he said.

Susannah felt stricken. She protested, "I can't give you a shot."

"I need you to do this," he said. "I can't let you go confront a menace without me, and I am just about paralyzed by the pain. Susannah, just do what I tell you."

"But, Leonard, I can't stick a needle—" *into you*, she could not bring herself to say.

"Pretend I'm a dog," said Leonard with a wan smile. "I know you can help me, Susannah. I believe in you."

"Did you have an affair with Michelle?" she asked again.

"No, I did not," said Leonard.

She had one other question, but at that moment she was afraid to ask.

The first aid kit was no longer kept in the lazarette—Susannah brought it down from the shelf across from Leonard's bunk. Dr. Tang had written a prescription for Cipro, and a series of morphine ampoules lay beside huge rolls of gauze, the container of codeine, and a packet of smelling salts.

The syringe was a slender, plastic missile—elegant, the sort of neatly proportioned arrow that could sink a ship, glittering and surprisingly lightweight.

Leonard talked her through the filling of the hypodermic with the amber-colored drug, the tapping of the side of the syringe to make sure there were no air bubbles trapped in the needle. He swabbed his own arm with disinfectant, wincing with the effort as he lay there, and then he held out his arm and said, "Pretend you're mad at me, Susannah. It's not too hard."

"Did you have an affair with anyone else?" asked Susannah.

He did not answer at once, and this, she knew, meant he had.

His arm was more muscular than she had realized, and she felt a shudder go through his body as she stuck him with more vigor than either of them had expected. She depressed the plunger, all of it taking place in a moment that did not seem attached to anything she had ever done in her life. She knew that she could shoot someone with the same air of practical urgency, the decision to get something done and done quickly.

She withdrew the needle and put the entire hypodermic back into the box like an unclean object she never wanted to see again.

Leonard did not meet her eyes.

"I love your mother," he said after a silence.

"But you were unfaithful to her," she said. She did not know why she was suddenly weeping.

"You don't know that," he said.

"You don't have to say so," she replied.

His voice was low, almost a whisper.

"Ask Martin to come here," he said, "so he can help me out on deck."

No, she would not, thought Susannah. She would not do anything more to aid a philandering husband, and she had no desire to help his stilted, self-serving wife, either. What she wanted to do was sink the yacht and every living being on it. Well, almost every living creature. Not the dog, and not Martin.

And not necessarily herself, either. She would think of something, she resolved. Some harm she could do to her father, and some way she could strike at her mother, too.

She bumped her head on a kerosene lamp swinging from above. Leonard had bought these from a maritime boutique in Carmel, expensive and cute, but fully functional. The kerosene sloshed, liquid within the brass interior of the lamp.

She had an idea.

This was more than an idea—a brilliant, one-person conspiracy.

She got an empty orange juice bottle from the galley, and a book of matches, *Ajanta Restaurant, Berkeley, California*, one of her favorite places for vegetarian vindaloo, a fiery curry. Being careful not to spill any of the kerosene, she filled the bottle with the flammable liquid, slightly put off by the very faint industrial odor.

She knelt by Laser. He was still sleeping comfortably, like they said on the news when someone was *resting comfortably* after a trauma. But that was probably almost always a lie. The injured patients were probably nearly always gaping wrecks. In this case it was true—the animal was peacefully sleeping.

And another thing that was true was: she was going to soak the money in kerosene and set it alight.

LEONARD WAS PROPPED on the deck, his back against the side of the vessel, while Axel and Martin counted the cash.

The potency of Leonard's recent medication allowed him to assume his usual humor, in a slightly vague way, and he joked that he was "morphine-ized back into the starting lineup."

But he nonetheless held his body as though something even more essential might rupture at any moment. Martin was grateful that his uncle had returned to help, but he knew that this current, reduced version of Leonard was vulnerable and that his pain would soon return.

Claudette held the pump-action gun, keeping it across her body. Susannah joined her, carrying a container of Minute Maid orange juice. Martin gave her a friendly smile, and she gave him a strange smile in return, deepening dimples in her cheeks but not actually showing companionship.

Axel murmured in the preoccupied way Martin associated with calculations, moving his lips in virtual silence. Martin counted silently himself.

They counted all the money twice, returning the full amount

to the gym bag. They left the bag unzipped, the money clearly visible.

"We have eighty bundles of hundred-dollar bills," announced Martin, "one hundred bills in each bundle. Eight hundred thousand dollars."

Leonard acknowledged the amount with a nod. His face gave no hint what he was feeling, only that the money had his full attention. He ran his tongue around the inside of his mouth. Martin wondered if perhaps the morphine slowed him down too much, or made him mentally fuzzy.

"That's a nice little sum," his uncle said.

"Why," Claudette asked, "were they carrying that much?"

"That's a good question," said Leonard. Martin knew that his uncle liked to acknowledge a remark, *good point, good question*, without agreeing with it. He looked at Martin. "There are problems with this money."

"What problems?" asked Axel. "I don't see any problem with the money at all, Skipper."

Claudette went over to Axel's side and stood beside him, as though supporting what Axel was about to argue. She had the gun in the crook of her arm, and her expression was somber.

"No law-abiding boat owners carry a pile of currency like this," said Leonard. He looked around, like a lecturer enjoying his audience. But he was a weary lecturer, and his voice was thin. "Isn't that right, Martin?" he asked.

"Probably not," allowed Martin.

Susannah held the container of orange juice up into the

daylight, examining the contents. The orange juice bottle, Martin realized, was empty. But not exactly empty—the jar held a clear, slightly oleaginous fluid.

"Of course we all know what has to be the case," said Leonard with a washed-out smile. "This is swag, dirty money, ill-gotten gains."

"We already know these people were criminals," said Axel. "They shot each other, and then they died."

"This is the kind of money that will get someone else killed, too," said Leonard. "Killed as in cut to pieces and fed to our friendly shark."

Martin knew what Leonard was doing. Leonard was a lot like his brother that way, clear-minded, independent, and contrary. Despite what Leonard was saying, he was going to end up keeping the money.

"This stuff is dangerous," Leonard said, reaching out and trying to snag the bag. He got his hand on it, and began pulling on the bag with a silent gasp. The bag stayed where it was, not easy to budge.

"We won't give it back, Skipper," said Axel.

Susannah set the bottle on the deck and selected a match from a booklet in her hands. Martin watched her very carefully.

She lit the match, but in the softest of winds, the flame went out at once, with a softly drifting, feathery puff.

Martin saw what she was about to do, as clearly as if it was spelled out on the Fox news crawl, *Susannah Burgess burns near-million in act of family terrorism.*

Martin went over to her, leaned into her, and said, right into her ear, "Don't do it."

A near whisper.

"I should," she whispered in return, no one else able to hear what they were saying.

"Please," he said. "Susannah, please don't."

"Susannah," Leonard was asking, his voice lifted in concern, "please tell me I'm wrong about what is in that bottle."

"You're not," said Susannah brightly.

"Susannah," said Claudette, "this is intolerable."

Axel was the only one who did not understand what was happening. "What's wrong? What is she doing?"

"I thought it might be the most excellent solution," said Susannah. She was in a mood of cheerful command—of herself, and her parents.

At last Axel got the point. He pressed a hand against his head, speechless.

She realized that perhaps the most punishing act she could commit was to let her parents keep the money and suffer the consequences. Besides, actually setting the money on fire would prove a challenge. The slight wind was enough to extinguish an entire booklet of matches—there were good reasons her mother used a cigarette lighter.

But she liked the attention, Martin getting so close and everyone looking right at her.

"Yes, it would solve some problems," said Leonard. His voice was just slightly ironic. "But then we couldn't donate the money to AIDS research. Or to help stamp out malaria."

But Martin's dismay convinced her—her plan was not such a great idea. She opened the lazarette and put the jar inside.

The drone of the aircraft was audible again.

The sound of the airplane did not please Martin, and there was new anxiety in Leonard's eyes as he motioned for everyone to be quiet. He listened to the approaching sound of the skyborne engine, and then he shot Claudette a silent questioning glance, not frightened, but measuring.

From the cabin, Laser gave a doleful howl.

"The noise of the plane," suggested Martin, "bothers his ears—the way sirens bother dogs."

"He's like a weird oracle," said Leonard with a breathy, unsteady laugh.

Martin was not comfortable with this talk of foretold harm, but he thought his uncle might be right.

"What do you think, Martin?" asked Leonard. "What should we do?"

"That's right, Martin," said Susannah. "We could put the money back where we found it."

BUT THE MONEY had mesmerized Martin.

He knew this, and yet he was powerless. He felt its hold on him as he reckoned what his share of so much money would be, and how amazed his parents would be to see him set the cash down on the family table.

So instead of disagreeing with Leonard, he asked, "You want to run with the money, don't you?"

Leonard looked at Martin with his head cocked sideways, like a creature looking with rapt interest. Maybe Leonard was surprised that his nephew understood him so well.

"All this argument," Martin continued, "is just so you can say we looked at every side of the problem. You crave this money."

"Yes, of course I do," Leonard said. "When I first realized what was happening I was worried, but now I think—eight hundred thousand dollars. Even if we share and share alike, that is a whole lot of cash."

If, thought Martin.

Leonard was even, in one part of his mind, thinking of keeping all of the money. He was probably not even conscious of the greed. It was a force in him, like the gravity that made planets go in orbit around the sun.

"He's right," said Claudette.

It was not too late, Martin knew. He could still insist that they should throw the money into the sea, or carry it back on board *Witch Grass*.

"Leonard's exactly right," Claudette added. "Fortune brought us this money, and we should fight to keep it."

"We might get away with it," Martin said. His voice came out of his mouth like crude overdubbing, his own words like some other actor's.

"Throw off the towline, Martin," said Leonard with a confident laugh. "We won't be towing *Witch Grass*. If they want their money, they'll have to catch us."

Martin had kept his mouth shut when he had the opportunity to tell Leonard that this was a bad idea. He had even offered that they might be able to succeed, support that he instantly despised himself for offering. Martin was struck by his duplicity and at how easy it had been to betray his own nature.

Now that the yacht was starting up, the propellers sputtering and churning, he perceived the determined slant of Axel's shoulders as he turned the wheel. It was too late to change Leonard's mind, Martin feared, and Axel would be adamant.

And they might, after all, get away with it.

Martin watched his hands perform their duty. He untied

the white line from around a cleat in the deck of *Athena's Secret*, and the length of high-quality, three-strand polypropylene stretched out into the air and drifted as the yacht found its power.

The line fell into the water as *Witch Grass* fell back, retreating from the yacht. Martin had to set his feet against the lurch of the yacht as the engines coughed again and gradually found their true timbre.

The wake widened and the powerboat declined into the various stages she had taken on, in Martin's eyes, earlier that afternoon. She declined from a crime scene to a menacing nautical shape, and then to the angled outline of a dwelling on the blue-gray prairie.

Axel set both engines at full throttle, and soon *Athena's Secret* was heading northwest at twenty knots, far faster than Martin had ever known her to travel before. The yacht caught the swells and rocked like a speedboat, the spray in the air sharp and fast.

Martin watched the aircraft as it grew closer.

THE WHITE AND RED WINGS banked over the distant outline of the power cruiser, and if there was any doubt that the airplane had been seeking the vessel and her crew that doubt faded as the airplane swept low to circle the unmoving vessel, cutting in wide circuits, the wings sweeping upward, only to slice downward again.

Then, with a swiftness and deliberateness that took Martin's breath, the airplane set a path directly along the wake of *Athena's Secret.*

"They're coming after us," said Claudette.

Axel was skillful, setting the yacht along a zigzag route so that the aircraft would not be able to glide to a landing anywhere close. The aircraft banked and climbed and circled far ahead of the yacht, as though the pilot was showing off his ability to predict where the yacht would be before she actually cut across the invisible point in the water.

Axel eluded this expectation, shifting the yacht's course.

The pilot was not to be deterred. This time the airplane was even closer, so near that as the aircraft circled Martin could make out at least two silhouettes in the cockpit. The aircraft's name was lettered jauntily along the cockpit door, *Red Bird.*

Martin waved, supposing that if the aircraft had friendly intentions, greeting it with a friendly gesture was polite and appropriate. And there was no need to completely abandon the charade that the yacht had only innocent aims, so Martin forced himself to smile. Claudette took Martin's example and gave a wave, too, voyagers out enjoying the Pacific sunshine.

A hand waved back from within the cockpit, and it was hard to read from this simple, back-and-forth waggle of a hand any of the pilot's objectives. But Martin could not help finding this gesture subtly mocking, like a fake laugh.

"You see, he's friendly," said Leonard, lifting his arm in the universal symbol of greeting, palm out, his hand empty of any instrument of harm.

The aircraft continued to bank and circle. The pilot looked down at them from beneath the bill of a baseball cap, studying the yacht during each passage, and the noise of the aircraft's engine was loud as it grew near, sounding very much like a chain saw.

As the airplane passed overhead, the pitch of the engine altered, a high-note, low-note effect that was almost pleasing to the ear, except that the aircraft now made Martin extremely uneasy. The shadow of *Red Bird* passed over the yacht.

After several circuits, the pilot released the yacht from his attention and glided away, flying close to the silken surface of the water, all the way back to the distant power cruiser.

There the airplane maneuvered, gliding and gunning its

engine, describing a wide oval, a graceful geometry that made the aircraft look peaceful. It remained there, not ascending, and not beginning its descent, a shape like a fragment of porcelain against the blue.

As it landed, the airplane came down unsteadily, its wings inclining one way and then the other, as though a new pair of hands piloted the craft.

The pontoons touched down with a shower of white, feathery spray. The aircraft touched the water again, rebounding gently, and then glided to a gentle stop, right beside *Witch Grass*.

"We did it!" said Leonard.

Axel gave a laugh, his hands on the wheel.

"We got away!" said Leonard.

Claudette smoked without saying a word, and Martin could sense her doubt. He shared it, all of this too real, now that they had counted the money and seen the pilot, actually observed him, a red-complexioned, craggy countenance, white teeth flashing in a smile.

Martin did not like that smile.

THE PLANE WAS DESCENDING.

Jeremy took the controls at Elwood's urging encouragement. "You can do this with your eyes closed."

Shako felt proud of Jeremy.

The two of them would go flying together when this was all over and Elwood gave Shako flying lessons, too. But they would have more fun than just flying. They would go spearfishing, off the craggy Na Pali coast of Kauai, down where the stingrays and the parrot fish held court among the reefs, like in the PBS shows Shako had watched. He had never been so much as snorkeling himself, and he couldn't actually swim. But he understood that there was more to life than he knew.

Shako loosened the laces on his Nikes and retied them. He cracked his knuckles and did an exercise he had learned from watching wrestlers, big men with way more muscle than Shako possessed, stretching and relaxing, moving from side to side, getting ready.

This was going to be Shako's day. Everything would be different after this. It was not simply a matter of becoming Jeremy Tygart's brother, with all that brotherhood implied.

Shako knew that he had committed crimes, and he had watched enough TV to be able to imagine phrases like *tried as an adult*. But he could picture an official at the Pentagon thinking that what they really needed was a quick young man, someone with specific weapons training. The Joint Chiefs of Staff or the Secretary of Defense would read about Shako somehow, and the generals would tell the cops to keep Shako safe, give him what he wanted.

"Jeremy," said Elwood, "you are doing great."

Jeremy was not so sure.

He was going to pilot the aircraft down to the sea surface himself, and he was apprehensive. Landing the plane was not like flying around. Not at all. Flying in the open sky you could survive even a collision with a bird. But approaching the planet's surface—that was different.

He was wary. He was giving the boat ahead on the water a wide space, not wanting to approach too closely, but even so he was certain that he would make a serious mistake.

A successful landing, Elwood had once told him, is basically a controlled stall. You fly so slowly, so very slowly, that the engine loses all thrust and the plane comes down. Right where you want it.

The sea was coming on too quickly.

"*Witch Grass* is riding high in the water," Elwood was saying. "So we know she delivered her cargo."

"What sort of cargo was it?" Shako asked, a rare direct question from him.

And it was a question only a very assertive or a very naïve person would ask.

"Mint AK's this time," said Elwood after what Jeremy thought might be the briefest of hesitations. No one actually spelled out information about what was being transported, or where it was going. "And rocket launchers. The shoulder-mounted kind, antitank, antipersonnel. Pirates confiscated the shipment out of North Korea, sold them to Mr. Tygart, and he shipped them to the California coast, or maybe Baja. Only Mr. Tygart knows all the details. His pumped-up deep-sea craft are a perfect cover—pleasure boats with a lot of capacity."

Jeremy had never heard his dad's line of work expressed so succinctly. He felt a mixture of pride and uneasiness. His father's business dealt in instruments of destruction, along with illegal drugs. The dealings were illegitimate and in some ways shameful. But if his dad quit, Jeremy rationalized, someone else would make money the same way. And they would not be as efficient, or as generous with bribes. More people would be hurt.

Jeremy let the airspeed continue to decline, sixty miles per hour, fifty-five, and still he knew that they were going too fast, the blue water a smear of reflected daylight beneath the pontoons. *Witch Grass* came on fast, too. Surely there would be a crash, the aircraft pitching forward and tumbling. He should abort the landing and try again.

But he let the aircraft descend, the altimeter showing fifty feet, forty—the sky, which had been a protective sanctuary for so many hours, unexpectedly letting go.

The last twenty feet took no time at all. The pontoons hit the water with a sound like crowd applause, an instant of ovation cut off as the pontoons kicked back off the smooth water.

Then the applause continued as the pontoons touched the water again and ran steadily through the surface. The aircraft slowed down, so hard that Jeremy was thrown forward against the restraints of his seat belt.

"Perfect," said Elwood.

He patted Jeremy on the arm and Jeremy was grateful, even as he knew that he was being cheated of something—he wasn't sure what.

The sensation of being on the surface of the water was strange. The pontoons had been appendages without any power—if anything they had been a drag on the aircraft as it sliced through the atmosphere.

But now they came alive, struts creaking, the sea working at an aircraft that was now transformed into a boat, and the shifting, uneasy, sideways movement, the constant slop of water and its swells and declivities was immediately impressive to Jeremy.

Elwood took the controls and taxied the plane, bringing them closer to the cruiser. Then he switched off the engines, a single act, but one that made a profound change.

With the engines silent, the propellers spun with a windy whirling sound and then slowed into a series of strobe-frozen images. Then the propellers stopped entirely. The engines had been running so long, and at such a constant, ear-punishing pitch, and the first thing Jeremy noticed was the deep quiet.

The hush was not faultless—water splashed and surged around the pontoons and under the aircraft, and the structure, airborne for so long, made even louder creaking, cooling sounds, as the engines, the wings, and the fuselage adjusted to this new edgy stasis.

Elwood opened the cockpit door, moving slowly. The door made a loud squeak, and the hinges shrilled as Elwood pushed it. He grunted, unused to such freedom of movement after hours of sitting. The rush of sea air into the cockpit was thrilling, tasting of fresh wind and sunlight.

Elwood climbed stiffly out onto the pontoon and held on to the wing strut, taking cautious steps. The big man swung his arms, stretching. He unfastened his fly and peed, as Jeremy glanced away, giving the man some privacy.

Then Elwood turned and looked back at Jeremy. He buttoned his fly and when he put a hand on the wing, supporting his weight, the aircraft shifted very slightly. He didn't speak, listening.

"I don't hear anything," he said.

He was right.

Witch Grass was too quiet.

"I don't hear the dog," he said. Then he added, "Both of you come on out, and bring the guns."

THE WEAPONS WERE HEAVY in the bag that Jeremy hefted down into the sunlight, hanging on to the wing struts to keep from falling, seawater slapping and bursting diamonds of sunlight. His feet squeaked on the fabric of the aircraft and the weapons bag was awkward, the guns stirring, shifting, heavy entities that wanted their freedom.

"Quick and quiet," said Elwood.

Jeremy, too, peed, and stood there breathing the salty air, a smell of hot aircraft engine and body sweat, the three of them out in the open after long confinement.

"Give Shako the Ingram," directed Elwood.

The Ingram MAC-10 was a large pistol, basically—nothing to look at. Jeremy had trouble fitting the ammo clip for a moment, but then the weapon accepted the attachment like a mechanism that had been to school and knew what was expected.

What Jeremy held in his grasp was a heavy T-square, ammo clip fastening into the ridged stock. The weapon was matte black, made for night work, and dull so sunlight did not reflect. A shoulder support could be fitted to the weapon, and in movies Jeremy had seen a noise suppressor on the barrel, but the essential weapon was what he held now, heavy and beyond menacing. Jeremy was fascinated by the firearm, but he did not enjoy having the death-ready thing in his hands.

"Give him the gun." Elwood was prompting with an air of genial impatience, but Jeremy did not release the weapon right away.

Shako was in the sunlight now, and he did that little wrestler loosen-up with his upper body, made a kickboxer strike at the air, and then another, warming up his legs. Jeremy admired his moves, a short- to medium-sized guy, compact, like a figure a computer artist would design and animate, Shako the Hit Man, not suitable for under eighteen.

Shako put out his hands and made that impatient flex of his fingers. Jeremy gave him the gun at last. Elwood had reached into the weapons bag and helped himself to the larger firearm, the Heckler & Koch, and now he put out one hand to the vessel and with an air of gracefulness swung his body up and over the gunwales of the powerboat.

Jeremy was alone with Shako. This shared solitude was a joy after being in the encompassing presence of Elwood for so many hours.

"I have to think of a way," said Shako.

He said nothing more for a moment.

"A way what?" asked Jeremy.

Shako had something to say—something urgent.

But the moment didn't last. Elwood was motioning, *hurry*.

* * *

Jeremy gave Shako a hand as they climbed up onto *Witch Grass*, and Jeremy was surprised at the smooth uncallused feel of Shako's grasp.

The three of them crouched, like men in a YouTube training video on how to capture unknown terrain. Shako looked great, a three-point stance, one hand down to steady his body, the other pointing the Ingram out into the blue. Elwood looked good, too, not as graceful but with a rough-hewn intensity, down on his elbows, stretched out, watching and listening at the opposite side of the vessel.

Jeremy had no weapon, and he felt his virtual nakedness.

"What do you think, Mr. Quinn?" asked Elwood.

Shako put his head down on the deck, pressing his ear to the planking. Jeremy was further awed. Where did Shako learn to do that, and how did he learn to sniff the air, like he was doing now?

Shako rose to his feet but remained at-ready, his knees bent.

"Both dead," said Shako.

"Go find out, Mr. Quinn," said Elwood. "And look for the kind of gym bag Mr. Tygart uses, a Sleeping Giant Spa bag full of something heavy. You won't find it—but double-check for me."

Shako didn't say anything, but there was an alteration in his posture, a silent *no problem*.

"And if you see the dog alive," added Elwood, "you know what to do."

Shako moved fast, his Nikes whispering, *squee squee*, on the teakwood decking. He eased his way up to the cabin door, steadied his weapon, and waited there.

He slipped off his sunglasses. It took a long, unearthly moment as he tucked the glasses into the front of his jeans. Jeremy admired his unruffled calm, getting ready, this real-time actual encounter with violence just another athletic event for Shako.

Shako blinked his green eyes, glancing from Elwood to Jeremy. He made that straight-line smile of his, but this time it was an expression of tense determination.

Elwood pointed impatiently, *go on.*

Then Shako slipped inside the rectangle of dark, the sunlight passing along his body like a curtain until he was gone.

Jeremy braced for the sound of gunfire, but there was nothing but sea spanking the hull and the moored aircraft gently bumping the side of the powerboat.

"What does that mean?" said Jeremy. "'You know what to do'?"

Elwood did not look at Jeremy. And then he did, and his usual ready-for-anything smile was missing.

"This is where it gets a little difficult for you, Jeremy," said Elwood.

"Difficult how?" asked Jeremy.

"You are going to have to do what I tell you."

Jeremy knew that Elwood had let him land the plane as a gift, a gesture of friendliness—a bonus flying lesson. But it was also a bargaining chip. Because now Elwood was going to do unpleasant things and Jeremy was going to have to help. It worked that way in his father's world, trade-offs and debts.

"Let me hear you say, Jeremy," said Elwood, "that you understand me."

Jeremy's own voice sounded too loud in this sudden peacefulness. He said, "You don't have to shoot Laser."

"I am going to have Shako kill the dog because the animal hates me," said Elwood, sounding matter-of-fact, even a little bored, stating what everyone knew. "And a dog with a bad attitude is dangerous."

The words sounded like plain speech, clearly spoken. But Jeremy was stunned. He tried to parse the words, considering the sounds like a scholar, examining the possible meanings.

Shako dropped low. His eyes adjusted to the interior light.

After hours of aircraft engine, this powerboat made faint but hard-edged sounds, overhead, underfoot, and each noise could be a firearm being cocked, a slide being racked, a safety being snapped to the off position.

Shako emptied his body of even more feeling, just as during the other times. Like when he met the Australian couple, met them in the sense of really encountering them, seeing that look in their shocked gaze just before.

He searched quickly but with care. He was ready to see whatever there was to see. He thought: only one. He knew this guy, too, that guy named Kyle. Just one dead man so far, and I didn't have to kill him.

He opened the fridge. The thing was packed. Shako took out a Pepsi and popped the tab, drinking hard. He blinked, the carbonation too strong, the stuff too sweet. He drank it all anyway, and tossed the can into a corner.

Shako put his sunglasses on again and felt glad he had not broken them. He used the Samsung phone to take a video of his face, holding the device at arm's length.

"I'm here in a place with a dead person," he said.

That sounded really stupid.

He started over. "I'm doing recon in the cabin of a big boat."

He played it back. *Big boat* didn't sound right. He and Jeremy would do a voice-over, re-record the words. People all over the world would see Shako, although he was sorry the video made him look green in this poor light.

He pocketed the phone. Outside Elwood was pointing again, a football coach flashing signals. *Check out the helm.*

Shako climbed the steps, saw what was there, and came back down. This was getting to be routine.

"Is Kyle dead?" asked Jeremy.

"YES, HE'S IN THE CABIN," said Shako.

Jeremy turned away, taking the news hard.

"How was he killed?" he asked, his voice shaking.

Shako felt strange talking about it. The way this sort of endeavor worked best was you carried the gun and at the same time you let words perish, all impressions fade, and just lived out whatever happened. Talking about such matters troubled Shako.

"I saw blood," Shako permitted himself to say. "No gym bag."

"I'm not surprised," said Elwood. "Our gym bag is on that good-looking yacht heading west."

Elwood put down his gun. He found a rope in one of the compartments on deck and tossed one end to Jeremy.

Jeremy had expected death. He was not surprised. But he was far more sad than he had anticipated. Kyle had been a Frisbee fanatic—Frisbee golf, Frisbee football, sending Laser out on long, arcing passes, Canine Super Bowl Frisbee. Kyle had been taking slack-key guitar lessons and had been saving up to buy a classic Dobro, a serious guitar.

Jeremy had not let himself think of Kyle—not allowed the

picture of his smile, the sound of his voice, into his mind. Jeremy had protected his feelings against this sadness, but now his façade failed.

He wept.

"Is Paul dead, too?" asked Jeremy when he could speak.

"Yes," said Shako.

Shako was troubled at Jeremy's sorrow. He wanted to offer a word of consolation. He had seen Kyle tossing a basketball, playing fetch with the dog. A friendly guy. It was too bad about Kyle. But Shako never gave himself over to feelings.

"We'll have to bury them in the sea right away," said Elwood, "and I'll need your help. It'll be unpleasant, but we don't want to speed across the ocean with two dead bodies getting rotten."

He gave Jeremy and Shako a few seconds to absorb this news and then he added, "We'll secure the plane to the stern."

Jeremy asked, "Where's Laser?"

Elwood threw him another rope. "We'll tow the aircraft," he added, to make his meaning clear.

Jeremy turned to Shako. "You didn't see Laser?"

Elwood put a hand out to Jeremy and took his shoulder. "Use a bowline knot, like I taught you."

"Where's Laser?" asked Jeremy.

"No dog," said Shako.

"Where," asked Jeremy, "did he go?"

"I didn't see him," said Shako. He was glad he didn't have bad news about Laser, too.

Elwood tossed the rope down on the deck and put his hands on his hips. "Did I tell you about that time," said Elwood, "in the Yucatan jungle, what I saw, dogs nosing around human remains?"

"Yes, many times," said Jeremy unhappily.

"That's one of the reasons why I hate dogs," said Elwood.

"I don't think that's why," said Jeremy.

Elwood was getting on his nerves. And he felt empowered by his surprising sorrow, and angry because he was sure that his companion had found Laser just now and killed him silently, with the butt of the Ingram.

"I think," Jeremy continued bitterly, "you just like to show off what horrible things you've seen."

Elwood did not respond to that remark.

"I'm going to jump-start the engines," Elwood said. "Then we're going to run down that pretty ketch and take what we find on her."

Jeremy wiped his tears with the back of his hand.

Elwood continued, "Are you going to help me, Jeremy?"

Jeremy did not answer him.

"Or," continued Elwood, "am I going to go back to your dad and tell him that some women on a good-looking yacht sailed off with his money and Jeremy did not do one thing to stop them."

Jeremy did not like to think about the money, being carried away at this very instant. Stolen. The idea of this theft was very objectionable, and it made him angry. He especially did not like considering what his dad would say if he was observing him right now.

He said, "I'll help."

But he said it in this new, post-successful-landing tone of voice, having second thoughts, grieving over Kyle.

"You think this is easy, don't you?" said Elwood.

The way he said it was scary, and it got Jeremy's attention.

"And maybe you think it's easy for Shako, too," Elwood added. "Jeremy, you have a lot of compassion for Kyle. And maybe for Paul, too, although I never saw Paul do a kind or intelligent deed in my life. You even have sympathy for a dog." Elwood made a gesture of easygoing reasonableness, patting the air with both hands. "Maybe you want to start having a dash of compassion for Shako and maybe even for me."

"My dad," said Jeremy, "would be sad about Kyle and Paul, too. And my dad likes Laser."

"Sure," said Elwood with a smile. "Reminding me that you're the boss's son all over again, as though I might forget."

Jeremy made a flick of his hand, impatient but acknowledging. Maybe playing the boss's-son note two or three times in an afternoon wore it out.

Shako wanted to tell him not to worry, this afternoon would work out fine.

Elwood debated inwardly how to force both compliance and good sense into Jeremy. A moody Jeremy was a bad example for Shako. These youthful hit men had to be kept following instructions; if you started them thinking and emoting there was no predicting what insight or remorse might derail them.

And Jeremy's monumental sulk was doing nothing to improve Elwood's own mood. Mr. Tygart had made a mistake letting his son fly on this mission, but here they were, dead bodies, missing money, vanished dog, and Jeremy about to get a lesson in how the world worked.

Elwood decided to keep it avuncular, even anecdotal. Jeremy had a soft heart—no need to tell him that Zeta was so badly mauled by the dogs that they found her lower jaw in the next county.

JEREMY DID NOT WANT TO HEAR any more from Elwood.

The big man looked haggard, standing in the stern of the boat, leaning on the rail. His unshaven appearance was taking on the serious stubble of a beard. His eyes were red. To Jeremy he looked quietly crazy and utterly dangerous.

Shako, for his part, had been thinking, maybe he and Jeremy would have a kennel someday. Beagles and Irish setters. A breeding kennel, with many excellent animals.

"I wouldn't hurt the dog," said Shako, unprompted. He felt this was what he had to say, and he said it. "If I found him, I wouldn't hurt him. I swear it."

That's wonderful, Elwood told himself sardonically. That is simply brilliant. Shako is vowing harmlessness on the one day I need Shako to be a piece of equipment that knows only one thing.

Because the rich people on that yacht were all going to die, Elwood knew. Shako was going to wipe them off the surface of that pretty decking, blow them out over the water, and they would be supper for the denizens of the deep. Elwood had to smile. He liked thinking about them that way, transformed into chum for the tuna.

"You are going to locate some of that frozen food, the two of you," said Elwood, "those Chicago-style pizzas thawing in the galley. You'll also see if Paul left me any of the Bacardi Gold, and then I'm going to get the batteries running, revise the connections, and see how much work I have to do on the voltage regulator. But before we do that, I'm going to ask you to please take the bodies of our deceased friends and drop them into the sea."

"I can't do that," said Jeremy.

Jeremy and Shako moved Paul's body first, the skinny remains with one steel tooth. The man looked like a stranger, nothing like the lively, nervously sketched stick figure he had been in life, always running off to the ABC store for Mexican beer and a fresh carton of cigarettes.

The body was still somewhat stiff, and they had to bring it down the steps to the main deck, and there was no other way to do it, no ceremony, no prayers. They rolled him over and dumped him into the sea.

Moving Kyle was more difficult.

His body made sounds, breathy, groaning noises, and Jeremy nearly burst into tears. The smell was bad, but to Jeremy the unpleasantness was necessary, the rankness of the corpse a definite reminder that an outrage had been committed.

Shako got a plastic bottle of Palmolive dish soap from the galley and a blue plastic bucket. They used salt water because the water pump wasn't working yet, washing their hands, and then they used a mop and sponges to wash up the blood, and that was the hardest chore of all, how the sticky stuff dyed everything it touched.

The main cabin was partly carpeted with Astroturf, and the blood stuck between the little fake blades of grass.

The two of them scrubbed, and a quiet work flow unfolded, a peaceful companionship.

"You know Elwood," began Shako.

This was an unexpected remark—or fragment of a remark—but Elwood was one of many things Jeremy did not want to consider.

"I guess so," he said, in no mood for conversation. He didn't think even Elwood really knew Elwood.

Plus, with Shako you might make a mistake and make a flippant remark, Shako might crush you like a tick, and Elwood and Shako together would roll your dead body into the ocean. Once you saw the possibility of such a thing you almost saw the logic.

"You know how Elwood thinks," Shako added, wringing out a sponge.

"No," said Jeremy flatly. "I have no idea."

"You know he has plans," said Shako.

Jeremy realized that Shako was being unusually talkative, and so he took a moment to pay close attention.

But the moment was over, it seemed, Shako taking the mop from Jeremy's hands. Beneath their feet, the vessel's engine was grinding, stuttering, grumbling into life.

"What kind of plans?" asked Jeremy.

Shako gave him that smile again, that no smile, thin-lipped look, his eyes shielded by the sunglasses.

But this chance to understand Shako a little, to extend their moment of teamwork, was important to Jeremy. He did not want it to pass.

Shako was closing up again, turning into the Shako who did not talk, and so Jeremy said, simply to keep the conversation alive, "What does it say on your arm, in Chinese?"

Shako looked down at the tattoo, a vivid violet on his lower arm.

"What does Elwood do with the killers?" asked Shako, his tone so level it did not sound like a question.

Jeremy understood that this was not a translation of Shako's Chinese tattoo. This was a broader question, and an insight into Shako's view of his own future.

Jeremy had considered this before. The youthful killers always vanished, killed in shootouts, surfing accidents, overdoses on liquor and pills. He knew what Shako was suggesting.

"I think Elwood likes you," said Jeremy. "More than the others, I mean."

But as he said it he knew that this was false reassurance. He was afraid that Shako would be disappeared, just like all the others. That was how it worked: there were videos of your target practice on YouTube, watched by millions, and you ended up gone.

"Elwood gave you a computer flight game, didn't he?" asked Shako.

A flight simulator, Shako meant, how to fly the twin-engine de Havilland, with approaches and runway patterns for hundreds of airports. Strictly speaking, it was not a game.

"He did," said Jeremy. He was careful, keeping the conversation positive. With Shako, you never knew.

"Maybe sometime," said Shako, "you could show me how it works."

Jeremy ran Shako's remark through his mind. Did Shako mean: give me the software? Did he mean, even worse, give me the software or else?

No, it was all right. Shako was just suggesting. He had the smooth manner of a killer, but for an instant Jeremy saw the human being in Shako, wanting to be a friend.

"I'd like that," said Jeremy.

FOR MUCH OF THE AFTERNOON it looked to Martin as though *Athena's Secret* was going to escape.

The aircraft and the powerboat both receded, dwindling into pinpoints on the ocean, and the wake of the yacht stretched far as she continued to bound through the waves, putting miles between the crew and the possible danger.

Leonard kept his seat against the gunwale, one hand clinging to the bag of money. Claudette brought out a blanket to cover his legs as the mid-afternoon breeze began to freshen. The wind was off the port bow, and the yacht was fighting not only the breeze but a current, too, as the sea began to work against her.

Under sail, she would have been a thing of beauty, but under engine power she thrust through the water like an extension of Axel's stubborn willfulness, and Leonard's, too, the two men driving the yacht so hard the vibration filled the frame of the hull, spray lashing the deck.

"Keep a course west by northwest," said Leonard.

If you did not know him well, you would think that he was happy. To Martin, however, he looked increasingly discontented, masking his anxiety with great effort. He sat on the deck refusing to look at anyone, staring straight ahead like a man waiting for long delayed bad news.

"Watch the oil temperature," he said, "especially on the starboard engine."

"We're good," said Axel.

But Martin was suspicious of this confidence, and he joined Axel at the helm, eyeing the control panel with its leaping indicators, needles approaching the red zone on the temperature and RPM gauges.

The only sign that their voyage might eventually return to normal was the reappearance of the blue shark. For the first time since the storm, the sleek predator shadowed the yacht.

"She's not made for this," said Martin. "Top speed into the wind for an hour is too much of a strain."

"We're good, Martin, don't worry about it," snapped Axel.

Axel's knuckles were white as he gripped the spokes of the wheel, and when a splash of salt water struck his face he did not bother to wipe it away.

Susannah made them hot drinks, cocoa for everyone but Leonard, who received a blue mug of coffee from her with a grateful smile.

Claudette leaned against the cabin, and when she knelt she was able to find a place where there was very little wind.

"No sign of *Witch Grass* following us," she said.

She handed Martin the binoculars.

He adjusted the lenses, and it seemed to Martin that, at

the very moment, stirred to life by Martin's attention, the distant vessel came to life.

Witch Grass began her pursuit, her prow a notch against the horizon.

Martin understood that the prevailing mood of his fellow crew members was apprehension—anxiety regarding the money, for the ship, and a dread of what might happen to all of them if they were caught.

"Maybe," suggested Martin, "the new crew of *Witch Grass* are a friendly, forgiving bunch."

Claudette slanted her eyes at him and offered a world-weary smile.

The shadow of the yacht fell back across her wake.

It was late afternoon.

Through the binoculars, shared among them, *Witch Grass* was coming on, determined and slicing easily through the swells that the yacht found daunting.

Even towing the aircraft, as *Witch Grass* appeared to be, she had an aggressive manner of reaching and maintaining speed.

Susannah came out on deck and reported that her patient was continuing to recover.

"I gave Laser some more broth," she said, the wind flinging

her hair all to one side. She used one hand to pull it back off her face. "His body temperature is back to almost normal."

She had put on a nylon windbreaker with a broad red diagonal stripe, like a tire track. Martin could see her in a few years, announcing to a nervous waiting room that the prize bull would survive surgery, but that the matador was now an organ donor.

She gazed back at their wake, a long laceration across the water. When she used the binoculars to study the urgent prow of the following vessel, she said, "They are going to catch us."

Leonard asked, "Why do you say that?"

"It's simple math," she said. "Our top speed is almost one-third less than theirs." She handed the binoculars to Claudette and added, "And I think I know what kind of people they are."

"What kind?" asked Claudette.

"Let me know, Leonard," said Susannah, not responding to the question, "if you need another shot of morphine."

He did. Susannah gave it to him, and for several minutes afterward Leonard closed his eyes, like a man dreaming his body back to well-being.

The starboard engine began to labor, and diesel smoke rose up, only to be quickly dispersed by the wind.

The yacht slowed, and their pursuers continued to grow closer, as though they sailed on an entirely different ocean, one that offered no impediment but simply powered them forward.

Martin could see Leonard about to make a decision, looking at his wife, and his wife looking right back, the two of them sharing a telepathic grasp of events. Claudette had a new way of field-stripping her cigarettes, tearing the paper away and letting the tobacco remnants vanish into the wind. This was not the way she usually smoked. She finished another cigarette in this manner now, and when she caught Martin's eye she said, "It was a mistake."

Martin knew exactly what she meant.

"Taking the money," she added, "was a bad idea."

Martin knew she was right.

"Ahead one-third, Axel," Leonard said.

Axel made no move to obey his instruction.

"Axel," said Leonard, "that was not a suggestion."

Dark smoke was now trailing out of the port engine, too.

"Axel," said Leonard, "I want you to slow to ahead one-third, in preparation for a complete stop."

Axel turned back to argue. "We can outrun them."

"You're going to burn her up," said Leonard.

Axel shook his head. "If we slow down, we're finished." He spoke in the simple, plank-like sentences Martin had come to recognize as the way he thought, too, every notion a nail to be hammered flat. "We stop, we die."

Claudette spoke to Axel for the first time in a long while.

"Axel," she said, "we're going to damage the yacht if we keep going like this."

The vessel slowed, pitching the crew forward with the

change in momentum. Martin stepped across the deck to speak with his uncle.

Martin said, "I have a plan."

Uncle Leonard was in more pain than he admitted, Martin could see that. And he was more worried than he wanted anyone to know.

But his eyes brightened when Martin approached, and Martin felt again how much his uncle meant to him.

"I'm nowhere near out of ideas," said Leonard.

"I didn't say you were."

Leonard gave him a playful punch on the arm and then caught himself, the pain kicking in again.

"You remind me of your dad right now," said Leonard. "Like the time he had to get me out of jail."

"I never heard about that."

"You did, too," said Leonard. "I tried to climb the Tribune building."

"Yeah, I did hear about that." It was a family chestnut, but not the part about getting arrested.

"The Oakland cops," said Leonard, "took a good-humored approach, and didn't book me. But your dad had the most serious look when he came down to the jail. Like all he could think was what was he going to do with a brother like me."

"What did he do?" asked Martin, sensing that as long as he kept Leonard talking the pain was not so bad.

"My brother," said Leonard with a twinkle, "gave me a smart nephew."

LEONARD LIKED MARTIN'S PLAN when he heard it.

"That's more than a plan, Martin," he said. "That's a strategy."

Martin opened the lazarette and set to rummaging among the emergency supplies. Sometimes, Martin felt, you had to act. He could even see the word in his mind, the way an instructing hand might write it out in red Magic Marker on a white, squeaky surface.

Now.

"We can outrun them," said Axel again, speaking to no one in particular. "We can break out the sails. We'll use canvas, and tack like real sailors."

"I always liked that about you, Axel," said Leonard. "You have a genuine fighting spirit." But he used the phrase *fighting spirit* like it was a characteristic you could live without.

"You need to believe, Mr. Burgess," said Axel, "I can make this happen."

Leonard waved off this remark, laughing forlornly, but

Claudette came to him and put her hand out, taking Leonard's hand in hers.

"Leonard," she said, "what is Martin's plan?"

"If they want the money," said Leonard calmly, "they can have it."

"So you want to wait for them to catch us? And then what?" asked Claudette. Her tone implied confidence that her husband had a strategy, but she wanted to know what it was.

"That bag of cash," argued Leonard, in a tone of quiet reason, "may be all we have to exchange for our lives."

"Sometimes," said Axel insistently, "you have to gamble."

But his voice was losing its power, and he was beginning to sound defeated. The yacht's forward movement had very nearly ceased.

"We made a good try," said Leonard with a sympathetic smile. "We have nothing to be ashamed of."

Martin worked fast as the others spoke. He spread a polyethylene sack on the deck and set the gym bag on it, working quickly and deftly, binding the container of money securely with duct tape. He threw in a handful of mooring swivels and other hardware to act as weights. He made sure he tossed in a working transmitter. He tied a loop through a life jacket and fastened the entire package to a length of polyester rope.

Martin could sense Axel's attention shift from Leonard, to where he was working.

"What are you doing?" asked Axel incredulously.

Martin said nothing. He strode to the rail, pulling the bag of money, shrouded and wrapped tightly, after him across the deck.

"Martin," said Axel in a tone of surprise and anger, "what do you think you are trying to do?"

"He's right," called Leonard. "Axel, let him do it."

"Do what?" asked Axel.

"I'm throwing the money into the ocean," said Martin. "They'll have to stop to gather it in, and that'll give us a chance to escape."

Axel looked stunned.

"And if they can't fish it out of the water," Martin continued, "we can find it later by our own transmitter signal."

Without any warning, Axel hit Martin.

He led with his elbow, and used it to strike Martin on the chin. It was an instantly calculated blow, and Martin felt it all the way down his legs, but he did not fall. Axel changed tactics and blocked him with his body, seizing the bulky bundle from the deck.

Martin was quick, and he hit him in return, hard, in the ribs. The blow did not hurt Axel very much, nor did it get his attention.

Martin hit him again, one blow to the side of Axel's neck. The effort hurt his fist, but Axel grunted and let the package drop. It struck off the wooden surface with a brittle, plastic, muted thud, and Martin wasted no time in seizing it from the deck.

Up until then, there had been a quality of angry horseplay about their fight, two friends who could struggle and recover with no permanent harm. That changed in an instant.

Axel pulled the Glock from his pants and pressed the muzzle to Martin's head.

Martin let the burden of the money fall, but otherwise stood perfectly still.

Leonard called Axel's name, and Claudette put her hands out, reaching for Axel and Martin but afraid to touch them.

"So what, Axel?" asked Martin.

He asked that single most nagging question, that open rebuke to any statement, however wise and conclusive. He had heard it in school hallways and locker room disagreements, the perfect retort. Martin had always disliked the obnoxious rejoinder, but now it was just right.

Martin said it again. "So what?"

THE QUERY BROUGHT FORTH embarrassed astonishment in Axel's eyes, but the gun stayed right where it was, pressed against Martin's head. The muzzle of the weapon had an iron, angry weight, and he very much disliked feeling it there, metal on scalp.

And yet, Martin felt unafraid. He had never experienced such clarity of mind.

Because he knew that he was either going to die, or he wasn't. His life had become very simple.

And with every heartbeat he was not dead yet.

"Guns are like money," said Martin.

Axel said nothing.

Martin added, "They give us bad ideas."

He slowly reached up for the Glock, although Axel's grip was strong. Martin squeezed Axel's wrist, and, inch by inch, he lowered the gun, levering Axel's arm downward as though he had turned into a bronze statue, frozen in dismay at his own violent intentions.

Axel's arm was heavily muscled, and he was stronger than Martin. But Martin had the edge that came from being in the right, and at last the pistol had been forced down across Axel's chest, pressed between them. Even then Axel would not release it. The two stayed eye to eye, locked together, and Martin was concerned that the pistol might fire—accidentally or not—and do bloody injury to one or both of them.

At that instant a physical shock, an impact from an unknown direction, made Axel jump, and his features twisted in pain. He remained upright, but he called out, "Stop that!"

This sudden, unknown force struck him again, and he staggered.

Susannah stood with the boat hook, and she swung it again at the back of his knees, knocking him down like a field hand with a scythe. He fell hard, and a bone or a joint snapped, a meaty pop.

She stood over Axel and hit him again with the butt of the tool, striking him on his chest. Axel's pain caused him to writhe, and that movement made him hard to hit.

"I wasn't going to hurt Martin," said Axel, reaching for the boat hook with one hand, kicking, trying to defend himself, and catching the hook in the face instead. "I was joking," he protested.

"You don't have to hit Axel anymore, Susannah," said Claudette quietly.

Susannah relented, but stood over Axel as a continuing threat. His nose began to bleed. He tried to sit up and fell back.

"I wasn't serious," said Axel.

"Go ahead, Martin," Leonard called. "Let's see how far you can throw that bundle."

The money was heavier than ever. Martin swung the weight

on the end of the rope, in ever-wider circles, the bundle humming around and around through the air as he gave the effort
all his strength.

Then he let the burden fly.

"That'll slow them down," said Leonard.

Distracted by the departure of the money, they all made
an important mistake: no one took the Glock away from Axel.

He kept the pistol, tucked back into the top of his Diesel
denims.

THE POWERBOAT CAME ON, breasting the swells.

Ahead of it, drifting like two connected chunks of sea refuse, were the life jacket and the translucent packet.

The money drifted, and so did the yacht, under minimal power, so that soon the cache of currency and the highly visible improvised buoy were far off, bobbing along on the swells. Martin felt very emotionally attached to this packet, and seeing the increasing distance between his person and the floating treasure gave him no happiness.

The figures in the pilot house evidently perceived this floating offering as they came on, like actors obeying a pantomime script. One of them leaned out from the helm and pointed, with nearly comical surprise, and it was easy to follow the stages of discussion, disbelief, excited hopefulness, then an increasing fear that this might be a ruse.

The vessel slowed down, the descending pitch of her engines audible all the way across the water.

The big man hurried down the steps, onto the main deck, leaned over the side with a boat hook, and he made short work of snagging the floating package and hauling it in.

* * *

Martin looked on, feeling desolate.

The powerboat was no more than a kilometer away. He had envisioned getting his own hands on the money again, or at the least escaping safely. He had expected that the powerboat would spend long minutes hooking the find, and even longer minutes establishing what it was, allowing the yacht to break out her sails and set a new course.

Claudette shared the binoculars as Susannah returned to the cabin to care for the dog.

There were three men on board *Witch Grass*—a tall, older man in the baseball cap, and two younger men, and they all busied themselves in the pilot house, not talking to each other, intent on what was before them.

The big man had a compact machine gun, the kind Martin had seen police SWAT teams use on the news. The big man moved easily, from the wheel over to the side of the pilot house and back again. The younger men mostly kept out of the big guy's way.

Martin felt empty and afraid at the sight of these armed men, and he looked to Leonard to offer further guidance. Leonard's expression was hard to read—he looked meditative, a coach running through his mental playbook. He did not look particularly afraid, and neither did Claudette. Maybe shooting pigeons on your own land, thought Martin, was good preparation for confronting people who could kill you.

Axel looked like a man ready to be hanged, his eyes narrowed to slits, one fist on the wheel, the other hand at his side. He limped when he moved, his knee badly sprained, or even dislocated. Susannah had really damaged him, but he rejected an ice pack, preferring to make a show of manly stoicism. His nose continued to bleed.

"Well," said Leonard, "I was hoping it would not come to this."

"You should have kept the money," said Axel.

Martin had to give Axel credit for being incorrigible.

"Shut up, Axel," said Claudette, gently but with an abruptness that actually silenced him.

Leonard dug into his back pocket. He held out his key ring and mouthed to Martin, *Catch.*

The keys glittered, and Martin one-handed them.

"Go to the forward starboard bin," said Leonard.

Laser was asleep, and Susannah looked up from her vigil beside the animal.

The cabinet door opened stiffly, and Martin tugged on a heavy green canvas bag with age-darkened brass buckles and a vaguely military feel to it.

"What is Leonard doing now?" asked Susannah. Her tone was disconsolate, but with a hint of faith in her father's resourcefulness.

Whatever this object was, it was very heavy. And its

heaviness communicated a fact to Martin, just as clearly as if he could read a label, a clearly printed packing slip.

He dragged the green canvas bag on deck, but the contents did not move easily. Cylinders and struts angled and straightened, rasping like playground equipment at a distance, a playful, metallic creak.

Martin opened one end of the bag. He tugged on a weighty thing, an object that did not want to come forth. It was cumbersome, wrapped in gray blankets, a mechanism of unknown nature. Martin recognized what it was with a mix of dread and excitement.

The tubes were forest green, almost black, and what were evidently legs to a tripod were the same dull muted hue, with fittings of nickel gray. He recognized the more obvious joints and began to fit the device together, like putting together a large, ungainly kit for a devilish child, or a team of demonic children, intent on malice. The metal was cold, and slimy with a fine, transparent oil. His hands were slippery at once, but the lubrication aided his quickness.

"What we have here," said Martin, "is a machine gun."

"NOT JUST ANY MACHINE GUN," said Leonard with an air of pride. "That, Martin, is a U.S. Army Browning M1917."

"You never mentioned it," said Claudette.

"Well, it was a little awkward," said Leonard. "Martin, there is an instruction booklet in the side pocket, in English and French."

"Awkward in what way, Leonard?" asked Claudette.

"Dad actually borrowed it from Paramount Studios," Leonard said, "to clean and rebore it at home, and fudged the inventory."

"He stole it." Claudette sounded matter-of-fact, not surprised at her father-in-law's larceny.

"Like I said," said Leonard, "it's awkward. My feeling had always been that any time Paramount wants it back, they can have it. I didn't want the thing—you know how I feel about guns, but Dad insisted."

Axel was looking on hopefully from the helm.

"This is a movie prop," Martin said.

He had felt a conditional enthusiasm, carried along by Leonard's optimism, but now he was having genuine doubts.

Maybe, he told himself, the thing would not actually work. "Does it shoot live rounds?"

"Live rounds, absolutely," said Leonard. "Martin, do you see that metal box?" he added. "Like a lunch box for a giant. Go ahead, open that up."

Martin opened the container and held up a heavy, glinting belting of linked bullets in their casings. He had not anticipated how pretty the ammunition would be, copper shells in an articulated belt.

"Thirty-ought-six," said Leonard. "Fifty rounds, and plenty more in the other box."

"It's an antique," protested Martin. He meant: Surely this can't be happening.

We aren't going to use this piece of trench warfare on people.

"My stepdad sells guns just like these," said Axel excitedly. "The guns jam a lot, but they're fun."

"Then you," said Leonard, with the patient joy of a teacher, "will be able to help Martin."

Axel laughed, a virile guffaw.

"You understand, all of you," Leonard said, "that once we fire on this approaching vessel, they have every right in the world to fire back in self-defense, and kill us if they have to."

"We don't know," said Martin, "that they actually mean to do harm."

"We'll make it," said Axel, with a smile, "so they won't be able to."

"I don't know how any of this works," said Martin, fingering what he took to be a swivel pin.

"It'll work," said Leonard with an air of cheerful grimness. "Do you think I kept this thing under wraps because I thought it couldn't kill anyone?"

The instructions were a fairly modern photocopy of an earlier printing. *"Position du trépied sur une surface plane,"* Martin read aloud. "This is awfully complicated."

Claudette took the helm and Axel fell to his knees beside Martin, wincing with pain. Now that Axel was completely involved, Martin wanted nothing to do with the Browning.

"We don't," said Claudette, straightening the sleeves of her blouse, "have all the time in the world."

Witch Grass created a delicate bow wave, approaching at a reduced speed. The big man remained at the helm. The two younger men were more visible now, and the smaller one held an automatic pistol, a stylish piece of geometry he kept steady in both hands.

The pilot let one of the younger men take the helm, and he stepped to the port side, lifting an automatic weapon of his own, a blunt, angular object he checked, fussing with it, glancing calculatingly from the firearm and back toward *Athena's Secret.*

Axel was working fast, his tongue between his teeth, his brow knitted. Martin helped, reluctant, but providing teamwork, the tripod up and ready, the gun almost in place, heavier than it looked.

"Hold the tripod steady, Martin," said Axel.

The distant, percussive racket from *Witch Grass* sounded happy, celebratory, nothing to be afraid of.

Claudette's voice was cool when she said, "Warning shots."

WHEN THE BROWNING was fully prepped, the belt of ammunition loosely fitted into the slot on the left side of the gun, Axel picked the entire assembly up, like an unwieldy camera on a tripod, and aimed it out over the stern.

Axel did not bother to raise the sight, a metal rectangle that lay flat on the barrel, or to make any further adjustment. He knelt behind the gun.

On the approaching vessel the big man lowered his weapon and was pointing, like a tour guide showing off a photo opportunity, look, how amusing—they have a machine gun.

But apparently the Browning was not visible, or its nature was not apparent, because there were no further warning shots and no attempt on the part of the approaching crew to take defensive cover. Instead the big man was lifting a bullhorn to his lips, and the click as the amplified sound was switched on was louder than the recent gunfire.

"Help me with this trigger, Martin," said Axel, out of breath with effort.

"No, I won't," said Martin.

"We'll just loose off some warning shots of our own," said Axel.

The two of them could not work the trigger, the lever emphatically stuck in place, like a device that had been designed to be immovable, welded fast.

Axel studied the mechanism and gave the side of the Browning a whack with the heel of his hand.

Electronic feedback sang across the sea foam, and there was another pair of amplified clicks as a switch was snapped off and then on again.

"Ahoy, *Athena's Secret*," sang out a voice.

The accent was that of a country-western singer introducing his next song. The voice was agreeable, and the words would have struck Martin as the kind of nautical quaintness that Leonard admired, except that the voice added, "Stand to, or we'll open fire."

Open fire. The formal quality of the phrase gave Martin hope. It did not have the rank bluntness of *or we'll kill you*, and so there was room for investigation. Why *open fire*, anyway? Why not simply *or we'll shoot?*

Another series of happy-sounding gunshots peppered the air and even when a series of humming trajectories made pretty, suggestive passes overhead, Martin did not immediately associate the noise with personal danger.

But Claudette was lying flat on the deck, and Leonard eased his body down, grimacing.

"Martin, the ammo belt," said Axel, "is not stuck in right."

Martin worked at it, and his untrained fingers must have made a mistake. The entire belt of ammunition fell out, futilely, sulkily coiling on the deck.

Martin tried again, and he wondered, in his mood of fearful mental clarity, what was French for *push the belt in hard*.

This time there was a satisfying click and the entire tripod shifted slightly, the heavy belt of copper and lead giving the Browning a somewhat lopsided center of gravity.

When it fired at last the M1917 did not sound loud so much as insistent, a maniacal hammering, metallic and not as ear-splitting under the open sky as Martin expected. The noise was like a woodpecker attacking a mailbox. There was little smoke, if any, although a pungent mineral odor was instantly in the air.

The syncopated, rattling *pum*, *pum*, *pum* of the gun did not sound like the product of an antique, but it did remind Martin of the stubborn ugliness of war documentaries, whiskery GIs with stuttering weapons.

Across the water, well off the approaching vessel's starboard bow, a stitching of bullets followed a seam up and over a swell.

Spent shells danced prettily on the deck. Axel paused, and the silence was abrupt.

"Good work," Leonard appeared to say, and maybe the Browning had been louder than it seemed. Martin could not make out Leonard's voice.

The era of the Browning's success seemed to Martin like it would not end.

Spent shells glittered, and in the late day sun Martin was certain that he could see the stream of bullets, whiplashing the water to one side and then the other of the approaching vessel. The pilot house was empty, everyone aboard *Witch Grass* hiding. Cowering, Martin surmised. He did not blame them.

But in reality the period of great defensive victory lasted less than half a minute. The belt jammed with still almost one-third of its ammunition unspent, and when Axel pried open the top plate and tried to free the mechanism, the brisk sound of gunfire answered theirs, but this time wood splintered and brass sang out, a discordant and shattering shower of pieces everywhere.

The stern rail beneath the Browning blew apart, fragments flying, and Axel cried out.

"ELWOOD, WHAT SORT OF GUN is that?" asked Jeremy.

The three of them crouched in the pilot house, the Astroturf-lined deck sticky with detergent. The machine gun sounded methodical, like an automated hammer, mad carpenters building a house out there across the water, and Elwood had recognized the clatter from the first shot.

"Something considerable," said Elwood.

He knew that the experience was entertaining, in a way—the rich fighting back like this. Elwood didn't blame them at all. It was exactly what he would do. He admired their intelligence and resourcefulness.

"I thought you said a yacht would be armed with shotguns," said Jeremy. "Maybe handguns."

"Have you ever seen me surprised before?" asked Elwood.

Jeremy thought for a moment. "When the frigate bird hit us."

"Well, this is another surprise."

He told Shako to return fire. Elwood reasoned that dignity—maybe even honor—required no less. Besides, he thought, these were not innocent men and women of ease. They had tried to steal a good deal of money that did not belong to them.

Shako hooked up the shoulder support and got a good aim, steadying the weapon on the frame of the pilot house.

Elwood stood up to watch.

The sound of Shako's Ingram was like a heavy fabric torn, a steel rip that took Elwood's breath away even though he had heard the gun many times before. The armament across the water, whatever it was, had been methodical and measured in comparison.

And the Ingram did real harm—splinters flew, and the gunner started and fell down. The human damage did not trouble Elwood at all—but the harm to the vessel was sacrilege.

Shako crouched down again, fitting a new clip into the gun.

"Good work," said Elwood.

But his voice was husky with feeling. Bullet holes in a graceful yacht like that appalled him. No amount of expertise could undo such damage, certainly not until they made it to dry dock and a skilled craftsman.

"Thanks, Elwood," said Shako.

It was the thanks and the smile that shook Elwood, made him see what was before him: a fifteen-year-old getting another clip into the Ingram, ready to use it again. Maybe Shako had just killed people with that slash of gunfire.

Thanks, Elwood.

Shako was smiling that tight little smile again, ready to leap up and shoot, but Elwood told him to stay where he was.

The yacht was silent now, *Witch Grass* churning ahead, and

Elwood did not need the binoculars when he leaned out over the port side. He could see the damage, white gouges in the pretty railing along the stern. All those hours gunning driftwood on the beach near Kekaha had paid off, Shako practicing his weapons skills, but Elwood was not pleased to see the destruction.

"Why are we doing this?" Jeremy asked.

Elwood gave him a shake of his head that meant: shut up.

But the boss's son had a point.

Elwood's dream of capturing the yacht, disposing of its crew, had not included the actual smashup of the boatwright's handiwork. Elwood would have enjoyed pushing a button and atomizing the rich people on board. They did not matter. But the yacht was a thing out of a dream, a seacraft shaped the way the soul might be shaped, if a human being could see the soul's proportions.

"Dad will be glad to see the money," Jeremy was saying. "He didn't say make sure to tow a yacht all the way home."

"We won't tow it," said Elwood. "We've got the plane to worry about. We'll radio for a crew and Mr. Tygart will send one out. He'll love this yacht."

"You're probably right," Jeremy conceded.

These young men were so quick to agree, thought Elwood. Even when they disagreed with you, they were eager to avoid conflict, wanting your approval.

No further volley stitched the water, and the yacht was silent, crew members moving back and forth. Elwood felt the joyful anticipation of all this ending, aware that killing the crew would mean more gunfire, more damage.

And did he really want to see Shako willingly and methodically, excitedly, killing people? Elwood had never been bothered by such feelings before, not as long as he didn't have to dispatch the victims personally. But now he felt troubled.

Thanks, Elwood.

Shako was looking at him from the deck, his back against the corner of the pilot house. He was ready, his posture said. What Elwood wanted he would get.

"I'll board the yacht myself," Elwood said. "With the two of you armed and standing by."

"We might not kill them?" asked Shako.

Or was it a question? Elwood caught an odd tone in Shako's voice, as though the fact that Elwood might change his mind on matters of life or death had special, personal meaning.

"Why," asked Elwood, "does it all have to end in death?"

Shako had never been asked such a question before. He looked at Jeremy, who was used to making conversation. But the interrogative had been directed at Shako, and he felt trapped by the query. Elwood must be testing him, trying out a trick question.

Shako did not know the answer to what had to be a verbal trap. And so he asked, after a long, deliberative moment, "Why?"

Elwood had his smile ready, a man who had been waiting.

He said, "Because that is the only way to get what we want."

A SHARD OF WOOD had hit Axel's forehead and stuck there, a wound that looked fatal.

"I'm OK," he said.

"Can you see anything?" asked Martin.

"Of course," said Axel.

Claudette knelt beside him with a towel from the lazarette. "It's not as bad as it looks," she said. "Just a very ugly splinter, and it didn't actually enter your skull."

Claudette marveled at her own calm. She pulled out the yellow fragment of wood and said, "Axel, tell me—how many fingers am I holding up?"

She was holding up no fingers at all, and yet Axel made an effort, squinting, counting.

Martin whacked the machine gun with his fist, but the weapon would not fire.

The powerboat continued to motor forward, less than fifty meters away now, and closing the gap until the two craft had to stand apart to avoid a gentle collision, the powerboat rising and falling on the gentle seas.

"So what is your strategy now, Mr. Burgess?" Axel was

inquiring, sounding almost polite, the towel pressed against his forehead. He could actually see now, after a fashion.

Leonard remained seated. "What's yours, Axel? I am entirely open to suggestion."

No one spoke.

Martin observed, not for the first time, how much more power Axel possessed when he was silent.

"We'll come to terms," said Claudette, ever the business-woman, and one who held a twelve-gauge shotgun.

"Of course," said Leonard, but Martin believed that his uncle looked worn down and defeated, his bleak smile an admission that they were as good as captured.

Martin hurried down into the cabin.

Laser was awake, sitting up and aware that some change was taking place.

"They're going to board us," said Martin.

Susannah was already armed with a cleaver from the galley, a gleaming steel hatchet.

Witch Grass eased close, and the two boats touched, the yacht rocking, the hulls grinding lightly together. Keeping a relative position with the yacht appeared to be a challenge for the strangers.

The power cruiser's continuing forward movement caused her to glide ahead of the yacht, and now the big man had to return to the helm and one of the young men had to approach the stern, with the same hook that had captured the money.

Witch Grass reversed. This maneuver was not easy—as the powerboat moved backward, she collided with the aircraft attached to her stern.

This entanglement was mild, with no damage to the aircraft, and it had even been anticipated—the young man used the boat hook with some skill. But there was a sequence of adjustments required, the powerboat angling forward and back, edging ever closer to the yacht. Martin had the impression that whatever the abilities of these armed strangers, they did not possess complete competence over the sea.

The powerboat was still having trouble, one of the airplane pontoons now rising up onto the stern. *Witch Grass*'s starboard engine rumbled, churning the water.

"HELP ME STAND UP, MARTIN," insisted Leonard.

Leonard leaned heavily against Martin, and then, as they reached the helm, he took hold of the wheel spokes, keeping his body erect with an effort.

Claudette was like someone squinting through smoke, although she was not smoking now, watchful but with no other outward anxiety. Axel was on his feet looking angry and injured, his head cocked to one side, the fist tattoo dark on his muscled arm.

The three strangers looked at them from the helm of the powerboat, a point well above the deck of the yacht. The young man with the submachine gun wore aviator glasses and had an unfriendly, set look to his mouth.

The other looked on with no apparent weapon, one hand on the wheel of the helm, the light wind ruffling his hair. He wore a blue T-shirt under his life jacket and met Martin's gaze with a nod, but not a smile. He wore a pair of black gloves, like someone prepared for dangerous work.

"Good afternoon," called the big man.

At the sound of the stranger's voice, the dog let loose a long, low growl from the interior of the cabin.

"Good afternoon to you," said Leonard. He sounded brisk, a friendly man with a lot to do.

These were people who could kill them all, thought Martin. He had never been aware of how dangerous his fellow human beings could be. And he had never been so impressed with Leonard, the man shuddering with pain but setting his feet, leaning on Martin for support.

The big man gave his name, but he did not introduce his two associates.

Leonard made his own introductions. "You have had a long day, Elwood," concluded Leonard.

"Yes, Leonard, I have. And it sounds as though you have found our dog."

Susannah was on deck, closing the cabin door. She carried the galley cleaver like a person who had been chopping kindling. She stood beside Martin and said, "The dog found us, actually, and you can't have him back."

Elwood gave a quiet laugh.

"That dog," he said, "hates me."

"*Hates* isn't a strong enough word," said Susannah, "by the sound of it."

Elwood tossed a line, and the white rope coiled loosely on the deck, no one wanting to touch it.

"Tie it, Martin," said Leonard quietly.

Martin was reluctant to let Leonard stand on his own, but he did as he was told. He secured the vessels together, winding the new rope around the cleat on deck, and then returning to support his uncle.

"But I'd appreciate it, Elwood," said Leonard, "if you would not bring your weapon onto our yacht."

The man glanced at his submachine, and gave it a what-this-old-thing? smile.

"A gun like this," he said, "can have a chilling effect on conversation, can't it?"

Leonard laughed, sounding breathy but putting up a good pretense of nonchalance. "A little, yes."

The big man handed the gun to his associate, the one at the helm. He said something in a low voice, and the young man adjusted a switch along the side of the weapon.

"But I carry a pistol," said the red-haired stranger. He lifted his aloha shirt so they could see. "Right here in my belt. I don't go anywhere without it."

Claudette stepped to one side, not in retreat but to get a clearer angle if she had to use the shotgun.

Martin had never been so awed by his aunt. But he could see the limits of her composure, the way she held the gun, her finger on the trigger. She glanced Martin's way and she mouthed *We'll be all right*. Martin was not exactly reassured. She was probably calculating how hard it would be to shoot both young men and then deal with Elwood.

"Take the clip out, Elwood," said Leonard.

Elwood let his eyes take in the Browning on its tripod, a hint that he found the machine gun proof of violent intentions.

"Please," added Leonard.

Elwood let the ammunition clip fall out of his Glock or

Beretta or whatever it was—Martin knew little about pistols, but this one was matte black and looked heavy. Elwood slipped the clip into a pocket of his cargo pants.

The big man descended the steps from the helm and called out, "Permission to come aboard?"

"Certainly," said Leonard.

Elwood waited for the two vessels to pause in their mutual, sea-driven waltz.

It took a few long seconds, and all the while Martin did not like the way the one with the aviator glasses gazed down at them, picking out first Martin, and then Axel, selecting targets.

Martin watched as Elwood got ready for the two decks to roll in synch, and at last he stepped down onto the yacht, doffing his baseball cap in a brief show of courtesy. He had red hair, spiky with sweat, and the aloha shirt hung down over the top of his pants, a bird of paradise pattern, orange on blue. His combat boots made shrill whispers on the wooden deck.

To Martin's surprise, Elwood dropped to one knee and ran his hand along the wooden planks of the deck. He picked up a splinter, one of the fragments caused by the recent gunfire.

"I'm sorry to see harm," he said, "to such beautiful teak."

In the cabin the dog continued his ferocious barking.

"It could have been worse," said Leonard.

Elwood looked at Leonard, his gaze going from Leonard's eyes to the way he was standing, supported by Martin. Elwood rose to his feet again. "Old-growth wood, I bet," he said. "The kind you can't get anymore."

"Let me," said Leonard, "offer you and your associates some hot chocolate."

They were speaking in code, a kind of chess match, increasingly friendly, but not entirely. If Elwood and his crew were going to commit violence, Martin believed, the bloodshed would have started already.

But at that moment Axel made his decision.

His face was a bloody mask. He pointed the Glock at Elwood, holding it steady with both hands.

Axel spoke the words as though they were pasted on a ransom note, each word separate and poorly aligned.

"We. Want. The. Money. Back."

Axel was tense—beyond fearful—and he was aware what a terrible gamble he was taking. This was why he spoke in such an exaggerated, command-robot voice. He was making a mistake, and he knew the depth of his blunder right when it was too late.

Martin felt Leonard shake his head beside him, but even that slight motion made him catch his breath with pain.

"No, Axel," hissed Claudette.

"The money," Axel insisted. But he sounded shaky now, riddled with second thoughts. "We will take it back now."

Elwood tilted his head with a puzzled smile, pretending he did not know what Axel was trying to say.

Martin realized once again how stubborn Axel was. It was a shame, Martin thought, that the splinter had not knocked him out. The late afternoon had been ripening into harmony, no one getting hurt, Leonard's good nature smoothing any lingering conflict.

But now Elwood's associates on *Witch Grass* leveled their weapons at Axel.

Laser had been throwing his body relentlessly against the cabin door, and at last the barrier broke open.

The dog lunged onto the deck.

LASER TOOK A MOMENT to bark threateningly, crouching and feinting, showing his teeth.

Elwood kicked him.

Susannah called out, shrill and sharp, "Stop that!"

The animal growled in a new way, a sharp warning combined with a blue note of pain, and then seized Elwood's arm, clinging hard.

Martin cried out, and Susannah grasped the dog's tail and pulled.

Laser hung on, blood spattering the deck.

Elwood had the pistol out, working with one hand, and he struck at the animal with the weapon, glancing blows.

Susannah cried out, and Martin raised his voice, too, but the animal would not let go.

When Laser did release the arm it was only to try to seize Elwood by the throat. The dog succeeded briefly. The man fought the dog off, but the animal did not retreat far, setting his jaws around the big man's leg. For someone in a difficult situation, Elwood seemed remarkably calm, as though he had expected this to happen and he had a plan.

Martin and Susannah had their hands on the animal's hackles, calling out, but the animal paid them no heed.

Elwood dragged Laser, the creature's paws slipping along the wooden deck. The man kicked at the dog with his other leg, calling out, "Shoot it. Somebody shoot the animal."

Claudette was ready with the gun but did not pull the trigger. Leonard was doing his best, calling, "Take it easy, everyone just calm down," like a cop trying to soothe a riot.

Elwood climbed up onto the ship's rail, pulling the dog along.

He sat there, fumbling in the side pocket of his cargo pants, pulling out the ammunition clip, working deliberately.

He was bleeding from his throat, his shirt front was soaked, and the dog had taken a piece out of his forearm. The injuries did not look mortal, in Martin's view, but a few more wounds and the man might well succumb. Susannah and Martin tried to pull the dog loose but the animal only set his teeth more firmly.

Elwood felt entirely lucid.

He felt that he was in command of events. He recognized the absolute justice of Laser's attack, even though he was terrified of the animal. That was at the heart of his feelings about dogs, and about the canine species in general. They frightened him.

Well, he would have plenty of time to reflect on all this, he thought, when he could apologize to these nice people, for everything. Because they did turn out to be pleasant people, perky if maybe a little bedraggled. Why did he have to work for Ted Tygart? Why couldn't he have a job with a man like Leonard and his gun-accessorized, stylish wife?

Elwood knew that he would feel great sorrow, not long from now, when he had to hose the blood and brains of these nice people off the teakwood deck of Mr. Tygart's new yacht.

The dog pulled at his leg, his fangs in deep, not pulling so much as wrenching at the limb, tearing muscle. The bites hurt. But Elwood could see the bandage on Laser's ear and sensed in the brute a residual feebleness from some ordeal, a quality of reduced power.

This was good. It meant that Elwood could, with determination, not only wrest his body from the animal's jaws. It meant that he could also, given a little luck and the continued dawdling reactions of everyone on deck, find a way to actually kill the animal once and for all. As he should have done two years ago, for chewing up a pair of brand-new boots.

Elwood had trouble fitting in the clip. This was the trouble with automatic weapons, always getting stuck. Give me a revolver, he thought. Or a knife. His hands were slippery with blood, and this did not help matters.

Well, he had still another plan. He tossed the pistol to one side. As the two vessels parted gently with the motion of the sea, he let his body lean backward, all the way, and he plunged down between the two vessels.

ELWOOD DID NOT HAVE TO FALL far before he hit the water.

He held his breath, inhaling when it was nearly too late and sucking in a little water. The brine seared his wounds, as he ducked his head under the surface and the two hulls gently nudged together again. They barely missed Elwood, but with any luck, he thought, they would crush the tumbling dog.

No, Laser was still alive. Elwood could hear the animal barking on deck.

That was too bad, he thought. His combat boots weighed him down, and his cargo pants were leaden, so he couldn't really swim very well, treading water like an entity that ought to be at the bottom of the sea, struggling instead to keep his head above water.

He worked his way at the waterline, around the prow of *Witch Grass*, all the way to the other side, and there high above were the two faces, Shako and Jeremy. Moving through the water required a great effort; Elwood was almost amused at his own quandary. Was this the worst trouble he had ever been in? Worse than that shooting accident in Oaxaca? Worse than that moray bite off Santa Catalina?

A lifesaver came splashing down, a bright orange flotation circlet imprinted with the name *Witch Grass*. Elwood hooked one arm through the flotation device and saw that he had to make some serious changes in his life.

Mr. Tygart was important, but he was a bad influence. Elwood would find his way to Ensenada, develop some gray market enterprise, smuggling people or liquor, bribe his way into new success. Or he would head into the Far East, carry passengers to Macao from mainland China, or fly poachers up rivers to shoot crocodiles. The world was full of possibilities. Elwood had become too limited. He had responsibilities to Shako. He could make the kid huge, use his talents to take over Juárez or the newly seething neighborhoods of San Diego.

The white nylon cord attached to the lifesaver was in Shako's hands, the kid worried that Elwood might drown. This was touching, one person in the world wanting him alive, for no good reason. Shako and Jeremy were calling—screaming, actually—words that Elwood could not quite make out.

His baseball cap was off, floating on the water, and Elwood did not like the way it looked, bobbling and drifting, reminding him of dismemberment. The blood loss was making him light-headed, and maybe he was going into shock.

Finally he could hear more or less what Jeremy and Shako were saying, pointing and calling out. If only one of them had shouted, the warning would have been easier to understand. Their cries in unison had been unintelligible.

Even so, Elwood was not completely surprised when the shark struck.

But what was a surprise was how much the beast took away, a big piece of Elwood, part of his side. Ribs, too, along with muscle. Elwood did some calculations and decided that this was going to be his last emergency. He called out for a gun, any gun, it didn't matter.

Maybe they didn't hear him. Jeremy was firing into the water, and Shako, too. The surface exploded, the guns blasting the reflected blue, and ripping chunks out of the shark. The predator changed course, vanished, and reappeared, bullets following the sleek silhouette, slashing the blue hunter with scarlet.

JEREMY AND SHAKO used boat hooks and hauled Elwood out of the water.

When Elwood lay flat on the deck at last he kept his arms outstretched, and his legs, too, a human X. The money was nearby, the gym bag surrounded by thick plastic covering, which had been cut away. The bag was unzipped, and bundles of money protruded.

"Don't," said Jeremy. "Shako, don't touch him."

"He wants to get up," said Shako. "He wants to get my Ingram and shoot that dog."

Jeremy noted *my Ingram*.

Elwood did not sit up, but used his hands to feel his own body, all the important areas, working carefully, taking a physical inventory. His side was half gone. His breath was making whistling sounds, out through the bony cage of his torso. He glanced over at the money and reached out for it, easing closer, until he could put one hand on the bag.

"Put the money in the plane," said Elwood, lying there on the deck and looking right at Jeremy.

Jeremy did not understand. But then, instantly he did.

"Take the plane home, Jeremy," Elwood continued. "You can do it, just keep the airspeed steady. You have just enough fuel."

Jeremy felt great pity for his flying instructor. The dog began to bark again, no doubt aroused by the faint sound of Elwood speaking. The yacht was already receding, the barking more and more far away.

Elwood died lying there just like that, like a man doing it on purpose.

Jeremy was stunned. He had never seen a person actually expire, and it was not like he had imagined. Elwood was still smiling. He didn't look at peace. He looked smaller, instantly shrunken, but in on a private joke.

Shako saw that he was dead, and he felt that he had failed Elwood. He did not like this sensation, the acid of personal blame, so he worked at the thought, pummeling the emotion, until he had a new sentiment.

Getting killed was Elwood's own doing, and not a blunder, either. He had done it to teach Shako. Shako wanted a picture of himself to record how he looked when he was learning one of life's tough truths, even though Shako wasn't sure what the truth was.

He freed his phone from his pocket and held it out, getting a picture of himself looking down at his late mentor, and then another of his face looking right at the lens. The intensifying twilight would make him look especially—especially something. Spooky, he thought, and—he mentally searched for the word—intense.

"Jeremy," Shako asked, sounding as unruffled as ever, and putting the phone back into his pocket, "should I shoot the dog now?"

Jeremy was upset and had to take a moment to respond.

As always, he had to be careful what he said to his new friend. He had increasing confidence. But this last question was troubling. And what was Shako doing just now, taking pictures of his own tight-lipped countenance?

Besides, both of them had experienced an opportunity to get off a shot during Laser's attack. Neither of them had used their weapons. Of course, Elwood had always acted supremely capable of dealing with any crisis. Even when he had called for someone to shoot the dog, he had seemed primarily unconcerned. Besides, thought Jeremy, maybe both he and Shako had seen the benefits of Elwood's possible demise.

"No," said Jeremy.

"As a payback," said Shako.

"We'll let Laser live," said Jeremy. "They're taking good care of the dog, so they can keep him." Actually, Jeremy liked Laser very much and would miss the animal. But he did not want Laser anywhere near the unpredictable Shako.

Shako nodded, unsurprised.

"We can still capture the yacht," Shako said, his eyes blanked by the lenses of his sunglasses. He sounded not excited, not hopeful. He was just going through his list of options.

"We'll let them all go free," said Jeremy.

"We could radio your dad," said Shako. "He could send men and a boat to tow it."

"We have the money," said Jeremy, keeping his voice steady, working hard to reason with this friendly scorpion. "That's all that matters."

Shako nodded, considering Jeremy's response. He said, "It's what Elwood wanted."

Jeremy did not want to explain to Shako what a bad idea capturing the yacht had seemed from the beginning. And yet in Shako's view maybe Elwood's death should be honored by stealing the yacht and killing everyone on board.

Jeremy could understand the reasoning, but he did not want to see any more bloodshed. He experimented with the phrase mentally first, and then decided to trust the words to do the job.

He said, "Shako, I'm in charge now."

Shako gave his tight, thin-lipped smile in response.

He said, "Whatever you want."

And then Jeremy had the first stirrings of a new sensation.

A feeling of power.

ATHENA'S SECRET WAS UNDER sail for the first time in many days, under a medium-sized working jib, the canvas lovely and full, catching the first hint of trade wind from the east in the ruddy light.

The sun was setting, bursts of cloud blazing on the horizon. *Witch Grass* was abandoned again, observed at an increasing distance by the crew of *Athena's Secret*.

Martin was at the helm, weary but happy. More than happy—he felt released from all that had happened. Susannah was with Martin on deck, and Laser was there, too.

"Brave dog," Susannah was saying to the German shepherd, a low approving phrase she repeated.

Martin watched as the aircraft took off from the surface of the sea and swept upward and then turned back. The plane flew in a ragged circle over the yacht, a wide, slightly unsteady circuit, and then it headed west, into the rising darkness.

Axel was asleep in his bunk, stupefied by scotch and codeine. He had wailed aloud that they would never see such a fortune again, until the liquor and pain pills shut him up.

Now, Martin could detect a soft murmur, Leonard's voice,

and then Claudette's, sounding relieved and eager to recount what had happened, turning naked event into another of Leonard's personal legends. For Leonard, money seized and money lost was nothing compared with escaping with their lives—and having a good story to tell.

Susannah was singing.

Martin had never heard her sing at all, and now she kept her voice low, confiding her lyrics to the dog. But then she was not keeping her song so quiet, and the song was right there for him.

Athena's Secret was alive under their feet, the strakes and beams communicating the texture of the ocean, through the deck, into Martin's body. The canvas strained the rigging, and the wind gently pulled the mast. The keel cut a space where the water had vanished, a space that the vessel sailed across as they soared.